JD and Me

A Southern Adventure Continues

William L. Garner

Also by William Garner

Me, Boo and the Goob: A Southern Adventure

My Circus, My Monkeys

Copyright © 2024 William L. Garner, Jr.

ISBN 978-0-9998916-5-0

This book is dedicated to the

Jonesboro (Ark) High School Classes of '74, '75, and '76

Dr. Louis O'Neal

Post 76, Marine Search and Rescue

and

Paul Grimm, Gary Angelo, and Joe Peters

Acknowledgments

A good book is rarely the product of a single persons efforts. When writers read what they have written, they do not actually read what they wrote, but rather they read what they were thinking when they wrote what they wrote.

Consequently, there are often significant differences between what they intended to write and what was actually written. In addition to that, there are mountains of spelling, grammatical and punctuation errors, too. Making sense of all that is what editors do.

Rhonda Sharp is more than an editor. She is a coach, a friend and a cheerleader. Without her efforts, this book would not be what it is.

Table of Contents

Preface

I have to get this out there right off the bat. This book is a Southern Memoir. That means this work is, by definition, made up a lot of suspiciously unverified events, includes somewhat exaggerated drama, as well as some very questionable people. This memoir is a roux of equal parts fact and fiction, liberally seasoned with healthy doses of exaggeration, fabrication, and outright lies. And a lot of what it is really like to live and grow-up in the South.

The story is set in Jonesboro, Arkansas, in the years following the 1973 Tornado that destroyed about a quarter of the town. This story takes poetic license to my teenage years. It is a representation of the reality of how we lived and what those years were like. Still, in keeping with the greatest of southern traditions, I've never been one to let the truth get in the way of a good story.

There are fictionalized versions of several people, including my friends and family, who are participants in these stories. You probably recognize one or two of them. However, a number of my characters are composites of two or three people, who I combine to make one character. So, if you think you are the basis for one of my characters, don't get all pissy because they do something stupid. It's not really that person. It's a composite.

There are stories and events in here that some folks will recognize, as actually having occurred. You may stop and say to yourself, "Now, that ain't how it happened at all. I know, I was there." Well, you are right. It probably didn't happen exactly like I describe it. That's because this is a work of what is, nowadays, called "creative non-fiction." That's when a writer uses real life but does exaggerate for effect, especially when…like me…they are writing humor. As such, it's true that I made a lot of stuff up. Much of my story, however, is true. If you think you are the basis for one of my characters and catch some flack about something that happens in the story, just explain to whoever is giving you grief that whatever it was that happened, is something that I made up. It is, after all, a southern memoir chock full of exaggerations, embellishments, fabrications, and lies. Or as Jerry Lawler says towards the end of the book, as you'll read, "So, this is a for real southern fairy tale because it starts with 'You ain't going to believe this shit.'"

This is a story based on growing up in Jonesboro in the 1970s. For the record, I never met Elvis Presley or Jerry Lawler. But we skipped class, drove on gravel roads and drank cheap beer. We smoked pot that didn't smell like a skunk. Our cars were loud as hell and ran like scalded dogs. We had the very best music and our girlfriends were really hot. I hope you enjoy the story. We who lived it certainly did.

William Garner

Raconteur

The Right to Remain Silent

Dad used to say that nothing grips a boy's brain quite as tightly as a bad idea. In the case of me and Walt, I'm not sure that's a fair statement. Sometimes things that turn out badly don't actually begin with a bad idea. They start off as a good idea, and sometimes for no good reason, things just go spinning off the rails. It's not really anyone's fault. Things just sometimes go bad.

Regardless of what folks have told you about all this, the story you are about to read is the truth as best I can recall it. I may miss a detail or two on occasion, but the major facts are all here. Some folks will try to tell you that I made a lot of this up. That isn't true. This is exactly how it went down. Don't believe those weasels for a minute. This is how it happened. This is my story, and I'm sticking to it. If you don't believe me, you can just ask JD or Walt.

This whole mess got started one night a couple of years ago when Walt came over to cheer me up some. That was a nice thing for him to do. I had been in a deep funk for several days because my whole life plan had just been flipped upside down.

My original plan, you see, was that when I grew up, I was going to play professional football. I had given it a lot of thought, and that was what I intended to do. I was a quarterback, a rollout quarterback. That's a good solid, high-skill position. Dad always said that I ought to choose a high-skill profession because you could always make a good living with a high-skill profession. Medicine was the best, he said. He wasn't real high on law. Accounting was okay. I'm not sure where he stood on being a professional athlete, but I did know that a quarterback in the NFL is a high-skill position. If you are an NFL quarterback, you live well and make a good living. That plan went out the window in just a matter of seconds. One single, solitary hit in a tackling drill at practice was all it took. I tore my shoulder up. I don't mean bruised it or banged it up. I tore up something important. I remember Dr. Manley looked at a x-ray film and said, "What position do you play, boy?"

"I'm a quarterback, a rollout quarterback," I said proudly.

Dr. Manley laughed a little and said, "Well, you were a rollout quarterback. Now, you are probably a wide receiver. Can you catch?" That was the end of football. If you can't throw the ball anymore, you can't be a rollout quarterback. Just so you know, it's not that I wouldn't play wide receiver, I have great hands. I could catch very well. I just wasn't very fast. If I was a wide receiver, I was going to be the slowest wide receiver to ever play the game. There are no slow receivers in the NFL.

So, it was game over for football. Time for a new plan. I was not real happy about having to figure my life out again. Truth be told, all this had given me a severe case of the blues. I was downright depressed. I didn't have a clue about what I was going to do with my life once I finished high school. Up till then, my only reason for going to college at all was so that I could play football at Ole Miss. Now, football wasn't even a possibility.

With football season finally over, and for me over for good, my depression just got worse. The end of football as I had known it was a heavy cross for me to bear. It was like finding out that professional wrestling wasn't really what you thought it was. It wasn't fake, but it wasn't exactly real either. Throwing a man around a wrestling ring is pretty damn real, but no one bets on professional wrestling. Understanding that changes everything. Understanding and accepting that football was behind me was tough.

Most nights, I just did homework. Sometimes I listened to music and looked out the window. Sometimes, I just looked out the window. It was sort of like being grounded but worse. When you get grounded, there is always a reason for it. I could find no reason for this. It was like I didn't know who I was anymore. I was lost, and I just didn't know how to find my way back. I spent a lot of time just sitting at my desk looking out the window. I watched clouds float past the moon while I thought about doing my algebra homework. It had not been lost on me that since I wasn't going to be a professional athlete, I might actually need algebra at some point in my life. I knew in my heart that I should have paid attention sooner.

So, Walt shows up one night at about dark thirty to "cheer me up." Walt's parents, Jack and Hazel, went to some meeting up at the Country Club and it was going to run late. Walt's older brother, Little Jack, was off doing something somewhere. Walt was home alone. Whenever Walt was home alone, interesting opportunities seemed to just appear out of nowhere.

Walt's father, Jack, had the mother of all Harley Davidson Gas Pro Deluxe Golf Carts. He kept it in a little garage behind their house that he had especially built for it. Jack kept all his golf stuff out there. It was a nice get-a-way for him, too. When folks came over to visit, the men usually ended up in the golf cart garage with a cocktail. It was a pretty cool little garage. Jack had a nice stereo out there, but I do have to say we need to work on Jack's taste in music some. I'm just gonna say it. His taste in music sucks.

Jack's cart was awesome. The cart had an AM/FM radio in it. It had a spot for a cooler and cup holders that swiveled and rocked so your drink didn't spill. There's a lot of drinking involved in playing golf. It had a nice little thing to hold extra golf balls and your golf tees. It had a place to keep your score card. The cart was made of blue fiberglass, had headlights, and little chrome bumper things that wrapped around it a little. It had a white canvas top with fringe and a lot of chrome trim. When you stepped on the accelerator, it instantly and automatically started up the engine. It was one tricked out golf cart. With the custom Playboy mudflaps, Jack's golf cart was easily the coolest golf cart at Jonbur Country Club.

Normally, Walt wasn't allowed to drive Jack's golf cart. In fact, he's not even allowed to sit in it. Last year when Jack first got the cart, Walt was allowed to drive it any time he wanted. We went all over in that cart. Sometimes we even used it to play golf, but mostly we visited our friends in other neighborhoods. A golf cart can be a really handy way to get around.

Last summer, Walt just happened to be sitting in it when a terrible accident occurred. Jack was going to play in the

Fourth of July Tournament and had taken the cart up to the Club. He parked it outside the Pro Shop with all the other carts and went inside for a pretournament libation. Walt and I saw it there and wandered over to it. Walt sat down in it and was generally relaxing while we visited with folks as they walked by. A couple of really pretty girls came over and started talking to us.

Walt was just kind of sitting there holding court because he was, after all, sitting in a very cool golf cart. Walt was just sitting in the cart killing time, talking with the girls. The girls, Suzi and Cindy, thought the cart was just the coolest thing ever. We were just listening to music on the cart's radio and talking. Walt had his arm causally draped over the steering wheel and his foot resting on the accelerator as he talked. We were just having a really nice time until he sneezed. When he sneezed his foot twitched a little which depressed the accelerator. The cart leaped to life, jerked abruptly forward. It almost ran right over Suzi.

As you probably know, golf carts can hit top speed in about two feet of space. There was about five feet of space between Jack's cart and the next one. The cart rammed the rear of the cart in front of it about as hard as can be. It was a very solid hit. The ripple effect was immediate and tragic. Jack walked out of the Clubhouse just in time to see the chain reaction collision involving Walt and about a dozen carts. There were a number of carts with significant damage and some very pissed off golfers. Jack had to buy drinks for all of the pissed off golfers and eventually pay for the repairs to the carts. That's why Walt isn't allowed to sit in the golf cart much less allowed to drive the golf cart anymore.

You should understand that not being allowed to do something has never really stopped me and Walt from doing anything. When you want to do something you aren't supposed to be doing, you just have to make some adjustments to how you do it or when you do it, and everything will be fine. We aren't supposed to go in the ponds for golf balls, so we do it late at night. Walt's not supposed to drive the cart, so he drives it when Jack and Hazel are out.

When Walt arrived that night, I instantly forgot about algebra and my blues. I'm not usually allowed to go out on a school night, so Walt left through the front door and I climbed out my window. We set out for the golf course and we were sneaky about it.

We didn't play the music very loud on the radio because that attracts attention. We didn't drive real fast because people notice that, too. We kept the headlights off and just casually drove up Mr. Walden's driveway to the gap in the fence that was our entry onto the golf course. No one saw a thing.

Usually, once we got on the course, the fun would start. We'd get going really fast, and then slam on the brakes and spin to a stop. Sometimes, we would drive really fast through the trees like a downhill skier. On this night, we weren't doing any of that. We were just going for a ride out on the golf course to try to figure out my future. We were just cruising around and talking. As Walt and I rode around and talked, my future really weighed heavy on me. You got to grow up to be something, and right now I had no idea what I wanted to be. It had never occurred to me to have a Plan B. Dad told me once that he knew from the time he was a little boy that he wanted to be a doctor. Walt had wanted to be an electrical engineer since he was six. I had known I wanted to be a professional quarterback ever since Archie Manning first walked on the field at Ole Miss. Now, I had to think of something else.

Walt thought I should be a doctor. He said that Dad could help me figure out how to do it. Trouble is that Walt didn't really understand all that goes into a medical life. There is a lot to being a doctor, and I wasn't sure I was up to it. He said I ought to pray on it. That's probably a good idea. I was just gazing up at the stars thinking about it when something came to me right out of the blue. It just struck me just like a lightning bolt. When I was a little kid, I always went back and forth on what I wanted to be when I grew up. I had wanted to either be a cowboy or a sailor. My two favorite TV shows used to be *Rawhide* and *McHale's Navy*. I suspected that life in the Navy wouldn't be near as much fun as *McHale's Navy* made it look, but the cowboy life seemed to have some merits.

I talked about that with Walt some. The more I talked about it, the more doubts Walt had about it and the more sense it made to me. It became clear to me that my future lay in becoming a cowboy. There will always be a need for cowboys. It was a high-skill job because you had to be able to ride, know how to rope, live on the range, and manage cattle. Rowdy Yates always had a job. Best of all, cowboys don't have to know a damn thing about algebra. You just had to be able to ride a horse, comfortable sleeping in a tent and able to count cows. You don't need algebra to do that. I could do that now. Suddenly a weight lifted off of me. I felt much, much better. My life was settled again and I didn't have worry about algebra any more.

Just as I reached that conclusion and before I could say anything, Walt whispered, "Hey…Look!" He pointed off in the distance a little ways. In the darkness of a moonless night, we could just make out a car. It was a big car, a Lincoln or Cadillac. It didn't have any lights on, and it was parked right by the green on the 5th hole. Walt smiled. I smiled. Clearly, this merited a more thorough investigation.

"Wonder what a car is doing out here?" Walt whispered knowingly, as he grinned.

We stopped the cart. Quietly, we sneaked up closer on foot. As we neared the car, we could hear something. Music, it was. We got even closer and could see that the windows were all fogged up. We couldn't see in, but from the way the car was rocking and rolling and from the sounds that were coming out of it, we both figured out at the same time just what was going in the back seat of that car. We were only feet from the car and even in the darkness, Walt and I both recognized the car.

Walt whispered, "I know whose car that is!"

I did, too. The only person who has a car like that was Mr. Maurice Adams. Mr. Adams was an attorney. An ambulance chaser, some would say. He had won some really big lawsuits about cars getting hit by trains or tractor-trailer rigs. He was really rich, but holy cow was this guy a pain in the ass. Dad always said he must have been raised by wolves. He acted like the Jonbur Country Club was his own private club and that everyone else, especially teenagers, were just a nuisance to him. He was one rude bastard. This was Maurice's car on the grass near the fifth green. And Maurice was, right now, getting lucky in the backseat.

I looked at Walt and Walt looked at me. Just by the look in Walt's eyes, I could tell that we both knew that opportunities like this don't often present themselves. Cosmic justice demanded that we take advantage of this moment. If we didn't act now, then karma would screw both of us later because karma doesn't like to be ignored. We simply had no choice.

I had a moment of inspiration. I had a plan. I love moments of inspiration.

I told Walt my plan, and we got going. We sneaked around to the front of the car. We stayed low so we wouldn't be seen even if someone happened to look up. The car was really rocking now, and the sounds were getting louder. I looked at Walt and grinned because we both knew what was going on in the backseat of that car. Walt and I took off at a sprint toward the car. Both of us hurdled on to the front of the car like we were Olympians. We were shoulder-to-shoulder as we planted a foot soundly on the metal hood. The sounds of our feet landing on the sheet metal hood echoed across the golf course like a bass drum as the sheet metal of the hood flexed in a most unnatural way. We were already laughing as we took a second stride to plant a foot on the roof of the Cadillac.

The idea was that we would run up the hood of the car, step on the roof, then leap on to the trunk and finally run away. We would then sprint back to the cart and take off for the gap in the fence. We called this "car hopping." You just run up the hood, over the roof, down the trunk, and disappear back into the darkness. It makes a hell of a racket and scares the crap out of whoever is in the car. We always thought this was hilarious. You would not believe the screaming and hollering that would go on inside the car as we ran away. We had invented this sport a couple of years ago and it was always a lot of fun.

On this occasion, however, it was during the step onto the roof of the car that the plan began to unravel a bit. Expecting a solid landing on the sheet metal roof of Maurice's car, Walt and I were surprised to find the cloth top of a convertible. This was an unfortunate surprise.

Of course, the cloth gave way and the frame of the convertible top immediately collapsed under our weight. All manner of screaming and cussing commenced immediately from underneath the wreckage of the convertible top. Instantly, Walt and I were waist deep in the Cadillac. We were in a life-and-death struggle to escape from the wreckage of the convertible top. The guy in the back seat under the top was screaming at us and grabbing our legs and punching at us. He was really strong. The lady, who was in there with him, was screaming bloody murder. This guy was growling like some sort of monster, and his voice sure wasn't the voice of Maurice Adams, Ambulance Chaser. No, this voice belonged to a monster and it sounded vaguely familiar. Finally, Walt got loose and took off toward the cart. He hollered back at me to grab his shoe. Seems that he had lost a shoe in the car. He wanted me to try to get it.

"Not a chance in hell," I thought. "I'm just getting out of here." I finally fought free of the man's grasp and sprinted to the cart. Walt had already turned the cart around. We had just started heading toward the gap when we heard, over the screams of the woman, the engine of the car roar to life. What the hell? That car had headers and glass packs! Who in the hell puts headers and glass packs on a Cadillac?

We took off in the golf cart at full speed toward the gap in the fence to make our escape, but before we could make it even halfway there, the car found us in his lights and was on our tail. We had to take evasive actions lest he run us down with the car. Quickly, Walt steered the cart into the dense trees in the rough along the side of the fairway number five. He was hoping to use the trees for some protection from the car. The car, horn blaring and lights flashing, caught up to us in no time and was right on our tail. This was not looking good, not looking good at all.

It might seem obvious that the speed of a golf cart is no match for the raw horsepower of the hot rod Cadillac's 500-cubic-inch internal combustion engine, but it should also be no surprise that the huge and ponderous Cadillac cannot match the nimble agility, tight-handling characteristics and dazzling quickness of a Harley Davidson Gas Pro Deluxe Golf Cart. Walt really was driving it like he stole it, which was kind of funny because when you think about it, he actually had stolen it. He dodged in and out of the trees just like Burt Reynolds or James Bond. All we needed was a soundtrack. We were doing pretty good for a little while, but then a low-hanging limb that Walt didn't see grabbed the canvas top of the cart. As the limb pealed most of the top off of the cart, the sound of tearing fabric broke the silence and the cart momentarily slowed just a fuzz. Walt howled as if he had been shot. I understood why. "Oh damn!" I thought. "Jack's not going to like that."

The car managed to stay right on us, running right over the pieces of the frame of the top that kept coming loose from the cart. The car was sometimes closer, sometimes further, but always right behind us. We were running out of trees on this rough, so we needed to cut across to another. We made our move. Walt cut over toward fairway number four heading for the rough on the far side, but in doing so we sideswiped a tree. Sideswiping a tree makes a pretty loud and expensive sound. Again, Walt howled. He might have been crying at this point.

Hanging on for dear life, I thought, "Oh man, Jack is really having a bad day."

I looked back and saw that one of the chrome bumpers had been peeled off by the tree. The big car just ran right over it like it was nothing. The other was dragging along behind us throwing up sparks off the cart path. I recalled that it had been really dry for a while and hoped that the sparks didn't start a fire.

"Crap, crap, crap!" I thought. "This is getting worse and worse." Walt was losing his mind at this point. He had been doing a pretty good job driving especially when you consider that it was a moonless night and we didn't have the lights on. He had done a real good job dodging trees in the night. Still, we had to find a way to work our way back over toward the gap so we could get away. If we could get to the gap, the Caddy couldn't follow us.

We exited the trees near the green for the 4th hole, went around a sand trap at the edge of the green and began a dash toward another bunch of trees. The car tried to cut us off. He blew right across the middle of the green. I heard the deep growl from what sounded like a Holley 4-barrel carburetor. The headers and glass packs roared as the Cadillac accelerated swiftly across the green. I looked over at the car. It was throwing two huge rooster tails of turf in the air as he tore across the green. He had a posi-trac rear end on a Caddy? Who puts a posi-trac rear end under a Caddy? The rooster tails kind of reminded me of when we saved Mr. Quarrels from his massive coronary a few years ago. Seems like greens always take a beating when Walt and I are in a jam. Mr. Quarrels, the greenskeeper, was not going to be happy when he saw those ruts.

The car quickly closed the gap and it appeared that he was going to hit us really hard broadside. I closed my eyes and braced for the collision. Just before he got to us, the car found the sand trap that we had gone around. If you didn't know it was there, you couldn't see it until you found it. This was true in broad daylight, as well as a pitch black night. The trap had a little bit of a lip on it, so he went airborne for just a second. We heard the motor rev up really high, then we heard him come down in the sand trap. We knew that this guy had just found the sand trap. We heard the motor rev up again as he tried to power though the trap. Walt and I knew from personal experience that once a thing with wheels gets bogged down in a sand trap, it takes a tow truck to get it out.

Somewhat relieved, we drove away at full speed. I looked back. The car was securely stuck in the sand trap. As we topped the hill, we could hear the driver cussing and screaming like a maniac. Again, there was something vaguely familiar about that voice, and it damn sure wasn't Maurice's voice. I was already wondering how we were going to explain to Jack the loss of the cart's roof as well as the bumpers and all the scratches. We were on the home stretch going down the big hill toward the gap in the fence that we always drove through when Walt looked back one last time to make sure we were home free.

That may have been a mistake.

When Walt turned his attention back to driving the cart, we were very surprised to see Mr. Hanson's dog 'Max' attending to an urgent matter of personal hygiene directly in the path of the cart. With cat like reflexes, Walt quickly swerved the cart to avoid running over Max. Unfortunately, in swerving so violently, Walt exceeded the capabilities of the impressive handling characteristics of a Harley Davidson Gas Pro Deluxe Golf Cart. Suddenly, it seemed like everything was in slow motion. The cart turned sharply to the left and began to tip up on it's right side wheels. I began a scream that seemed to echo in my head as my side of the cart lifted high into the air. I lost my balance and was about to fall from the cart when I reached desperately for a hand hold. I got a grip on a flapping remnant of the canvas cart top while Walt fought valiantly to regain control of the cart and not let it flip completely over. He might have been successful had the remnant of roof not torn away and allowed me to fall from the cart. This significantly altered the center of balance of the cart. With my weight no longer a balancing factor, the cart quickly flipped. Walt was flung free on the first flip. The cart continued bounding down the fairway like a NASCAR race car flipping down the track. On about the third bounce, it burst into flames. Gas from the gas tank must have found a spark. The cart was a flaming snowball bouncing down the steep hill of the fairway. It's blazing journey finally ended in the shallows of the pond at the bottom of the hill.

Walt and I were in shock. We just sat there in the grass of the fairway looking at the burning wreckage of Jack's pride and joy. The cart made so much noise when it cartwheeled down the fairway that lights were coming on in the backyards of some of the houses along the fairway. The impact of being thrown from the cart knocked the wind out of Walt. He staggered around a couple of minutes turning blue while he tried to breathe again. I could see people in their backyards looking into the fairway trying to see what was going on. All the 'action' was down at the pond, so no one looked at us in the fairway.

"Good thing it was dark," I thought to myself. "They probably couldn't see us if they looked."

Finally, we both sat down in the grass of the fairway. Walt thought he had broken some ribs. I had him spit in my hand. I checked, no blood in his spit. I told him he would live. For a while, we just looked at the golf cart burning in the pond. The cart was a disaster. With its AM/FM radio, the cooler and cup holders, the nice little thing to hold extra golf balls and your tees and the place to keep your score card, it was a great golf cart. Jack used to wax it as if it were a sports car. With the wail of approaching sirens piercing the peaceful silence of the night, we looked at the flames reflecting on the water. There was a surreal beauty to it all. We, nonetheless, were dumbfounded. How in the hell does a casual drive around a golf course on a golf cart end like this?

Oh, this was bad and getting worse by the minute. Just now we could see police lights in one of the other fairways heading toward the sand trap. Soon they would come to investigate the fire the cart had started in the fairway. It was time for us to go. We set out walking home. It took a minute to wrap our brains around what had happened. It was clear to us that there was no way out of this. After a brief discussion, we concluded that we ought to just be honest and just tell Jack the truth about what had happened. There are times when honesty is the best policy. We knew that he probably wouldn't understand, but it seemed like the truth was going to be the best way to go.

Realizing this, Walt looked for all the world like a condemned man. He knew that Jack would not understand what had happened at all. Sometimes bad things just happen, that's life. No way would Jack understand this. Walt fully expected that, if Jack didn't put him up for adoption, he would at least make his life miserable forever. Walt was just stuck. He just looked down at his feet, as we slowly walked home. Both of us knew Walt was doomed, but I also knew that there was no way Walt could take the fall for this all by himself. He would give me up in a heartbeat. My mind raced. Surely there was an out. There had to be some way we could make this better or at least not as bad. The cart was a complete wreck. It was a burning corpse, lying smashed in a water hazard on the back side of the front nine. I hoped the fire wouldn't spread beyond the one fairway. The car, the cops and some maniac, were all out at the sand trap. This was really, really, really bad, and then, suddenly, I had an epiphany.

"You know," I reminded Walt, "no one knows that we were out on the cart tonight." Walt perked up a little. "If no one knows we were on the cart," I said, "and we don't say anything, then no one will know we were involved at all. We don't have to say anything to anyone about anything. We don't have to lie or nothing."

Walt looked at me in disbelief and said, "But my shoe…"

"Don't worry about the damn shoe! Your shoe isn't the problem and it won't be a problem," I said. "Let's just go home, go to bed, and not say a word," I said. I was a little surprised that on a night when we had just destroyed his father's golf cart he would be worried about some damn shoe.

Walt thought for a second and then, for the first time since we had wrecked the cart, Walt smiled. We didn't have to lie. Walt didn't like lying. The whole burn-in-hell thing always hung him up. We just had to stay quiet and all would be fine. This was a great solution. We'd stay quiet and it would all blow over. We walked a little faster going home. Perhaps we weren't doomed after all. Tomorrow would be a great day after all.

And that's exactly what we did. We went home, got in bed, and went to sleep. In the morning, we got up, just like nothing had happened and went to school. No problem. It must have appeared that we didn't have a worry in the world. Well, no worries until Jack got home.

I don't know when Mr. Quarrels, the greenskeeper at the Country Club, discovered the wrecked golf cart. When he looked at the cart, I'm sure he knew right away whose it was. There was only one Harley Davidson Gas Pro Deluxe Golf Cart with Playboy mud flaps at the Country Club.

Walt said when his father got home that night he was beyond angry. Mr Quarrels had called him at about nine in the morning. Jack went to the club to see his cart. It was totaled. According to Mr. Quarrels, not even the wheels could be salvaged off of the cart. Everything was a mess. Mr. Quarrels knew it was Joe's cart because one of the mud flaps survived the fire. Walt said that while his father was telling his mother all this, he just sat quiet and did not even move. At no point did his father ever look at him or suspect him of involvement. Just like we thought, this was working out. It was going to be okay.

Walt's older brother, Little Jack, was a big fan of professional wrestling. On Friday nights professional wrestling was held in the American Legion Arena down by the hospital. Little Jack loved to go to the matches. Sometimes Walt would go with him. On this occasion, just to get away from Jack and out of the house while Jack vented a little more about the cart, Walt went to the wrestling match with Little Jack. Staying home, he said, was just too stressful.

On Saturday morning while I was eating breakfast, Walt called. I could tell something was up from his voice. I stretched the phone cord so that I could stand around the corner from the kitchen and talk in semi-privacy.

"What's wrong?" I asked.

"You are not going to believe it. We're going to die," he said, almost crying.

"What? Tell me!" I whispered as hard as I could. "What is it?" I implored.

"Oh, it's bad! It's so bad!" he whispered with desperation sneaking into his voice.

"What's bad? Is it about the 'thing?'" I whispered referencing our adventures of the other night.

"Oh yeah! You won't believe it. That sure wasn't Maurice's car, you know, but you'll never guess whose car that was on the golf course. You'll never, ever, ever guess whose car it was," he said sounding like he had just seen the Wicked Witch of the West.

"What? Dammit! Quit screwing around! Tell me!" I said. I was getting impatient and almost speaking too loud.

"The car that got stuck in the sand trap…" Walt said.

"Yeah, it wasn't Maurice's car. We knew that," I said impatiently. "Who was in the car?"

"Jerry Lawler," he said.

"Who? Jerry Lawler? The King, Jerry Lawler?" I asked. I remembered hearing the voice last night and realized that indeed it was Jerry Lawler's voice. I heard him talking with Lance Russell and Dave Brown on Mid-South Wrestling nearly every Saturday morning. I had a sinking feeling in the pit of my stomach.

"Yes," came the clearly freighted answer. "Jerry Lawler! Mid-America Wrestling Federation's Heavy Weight World Champion Jerry Lawler!"

"It was Jerry Lawler's car! And he had Little Jack's shoe at the match," Walt whispered almost crying, "and he's not a happy man! He's not a happy man at all. Right there in the middle of the ring, he offered a reward for someone to turn in the yellow little bastards who wrecked his top. Jerry says we can run but we cannot hide. He's going to find us, and after he finds us, no one will ever find us again. Then, you know what he did? He tore the shoe in half. He tore Little Jack's blue-suede Converse sneaker clean in half. This is the end of the world."

"Little Jack's shoe?" I asked. "How'd he get Little Jack's shoe?"

"Those were Little Jack's blue-suede Converse tennis shoes I was wearing," Walt replied.

"Calm down, it's okay," I told him. "We are the only ones who know what happened. There's no one to rat us out," I assured Walt in a calm voice. "It will be okay," I said.

There was silence for a minute.

Finally, Walt said, "Little Jack knows."

Damn.

So, you can see how quickly things can fall apart on you. Good ideas can go off the rails in a half a second. It's not really anyone's fault. Bad things just happen. One minute you are just trying to work things out and stay on the good side of karma, and the next minute you are on a golf cart in a race for your life across a golf course in pitch black darkness. Just when you think it can't get worse, you find out that it can. It can get a lot worse.

As fate would have it, Little Jack wasn't the only one who knew about our adventure. Mr. Parker had heard the music from the radio on the cart and had seen us go by his house on the way to the golf course. Mr. Walden had seen us go up his driveway to get to the gap in the fence to get onto the golf course, and Mrs. Frazier had seen us when we were walking home after wrecking the golf cart. She noticed Walt was limping because he only had one shoe on. Of course, there were all those folks who turned their lights on and went out into their backyards when they heard the crash and saw the fire. Seems the lights from their back porches reach pretty far out into the fairway and they all saw me and Walt. I think it was the police cars out on the golf course that tipped them off that we had been involved in something more than just a cart crash.

By the time Mr Quarrels called Jack to tell him that the shattered, burned out, lifeless hulk, of his beloved golf cart had been found smoldering in the shallow waters of a minor water hazard on the fourth fairway, nearly everyone in the neighborhood already knew that Walt and I had wrecked Jack's golf cart out on the golf course at about nine-thirty the night before, while we were getting chased across the golf course by a pissed off professional wrestler driving a souped-up Cadillac with a demolished convertible top. The cart exploding and setting the fairway on fire was just the icing on the cake.

Well, staying quiet just wasn't going to work for us this time.

Ducks Unlimited

Just in case you don't know, Jerry Lawler is a professional wrestler from Memphis. He's on TV nearly every Saturday. He is always at the big wrestling events they have at the coliseum. I'm not a big fan, so I don't go to the wrestling matches, but Walt has been several times. When Jerry Lawler first started wrestling, he was a bad guy. Over time, he became a good guy and today he is one of the most popular wrestlers in the world. Nonetheless, I have seen him pick a guy up and throw him out of the ring like he was a Frisbee. Everyone knows that once you make Jerry mad, you are done. Once he yanks that strap off of his shoulder, everyone knows that it's all over but the crying. When he yanks that strap it is a sign that someone is about to get their butt beat. It is that Jerry Lawler who we had to apologize to. I was pretty sure we had already made him mad.

Dad and Jack called over to Mr. Lawler's office in Memphis and made arrangements for me and Walt to go over to Memphis to apologize to him and to make arrangements to pay for the damage we caused. That was a big thing with Dad and Jack. If you break something, you have to make it right.

The drive to Memphis was long, slow drive. Neither one of us wanted to go. We knew what happened to people who made Jerry Lawler mad. Jerry was never one to cheat and hit a guy with a chair, but he would throw a person up in the air and drop kick him on the way down. I don't care how "fixed" professional wrestling might be, getting drop kicked like that has to hurt.

Mr. Lawler's office was on the 16th floor of the Sterick Building in downtown Memphis. We parked on the street and took the elevator up to the 16th floor. I looked out the window by the elevators. I could see the Memphis/Arkansas Bridge in the distance. The Mississippi River ran beneath it. I would rather jump off the bridge than go through the door marked "Mid-America Wrestling." Walt and I were scared to death. After pausing for a long, nervous few seconds, I looked at Walt and he looked at me. Neither of us wanted to open the door. I was pretty sure I would rather French kiss a monkey's ass than open that door, but finally we did. We opened it and walked through that door into the holy of holys of professional wrestling, the general offices of Mid-America Wrestling.

Let me tell you, Mr. Lawler is a very large, very intense man. I swear he growled real low when we walked into his office. (Who knew wrestlers had offices?) When we apologized, I was scared to death. We had to look him straight in the eye and tell him how sorry we were that we had destroyed the top to his car. I figured it was a good idea not to mention what he was doing in the backseat when we destroyed his roof. We brought a paper that Walt's dad had typed up for us. It said we would repair his car and pay for having it pulled out of the sand trap. My knees were knocking when Walt handed the paper to Mr. Lawler. He growled again as he read it. He looked up slowly. He looked at me, then at Walt. He tore the paper up and threw it in the trash can. He came out from behind the desk, and my life began to flash before my eyes. I just knew that this was going to be the part of the meeting when Walt and I get our asses beat. I figured he was about to rip his shirt off and start throwing us around the office like that gorilla in the Samsonite luggage commercial does the luggage at the airport. Jerry Lawler must have weighed 250 pounds of solid muscle. He stood right in front of me looking at me as if I were a chew toy. I was hyperventilating. I was getting dizzy.

"We don't need a stupid piece of paper," he growled. "Men shake hands on a deal." He stuck out the biggest hand I have ever seen on a human being. "Oh dear God," I thought. "I'm a dead man."

"Papers are for lawyers," he snarled. He sniffed the air and fixed a steely gaze on me. "You don't smell like no stinking lawyer."

He wanted to look us straight in the eye and get a handshake. I looked at him and I felt like I was looking up at the Lincoln Memorial. Jerry Lawler is a big guy, a really big guy. When we shook hands, I worried that he might squeeze my hand real hard just to make a point, but he didn't. He just looked me straight in the eye. He had black, dangerous eyes. He gave me a firm handshake, and said in a really, really tough voice, almost a growl, "Okay kid, we got a deal." I couldn't be sure, but I swear I thought I saw a little hint of a smile.

He did the same thing with Walt. It is a major understatement to say that we were greatly relieved when this was all over. Dad cosigned a note at the bank for me and Walt. We had Mr. Lawler's car top repaired and paid for the tow truck. I would be very happy if I never saw him up close and personal ever again.

Jack was a little harder to deal with. Jack really took the cart crash hard. Due to the fire, the cart was a total loss. Dad said Jack was traumatized. Before we could buy him a new cart, Jack had the right to chew our butts for a while. When I say "a while," I mean a few weeks. Jack just had to get it out of his system. I'm sure you know how it is when you are really angry like that. It just takes a while to get over it. Eventually, we bought Jack a new golf cart with all the bells and whistles. Jack cosigned another note up at the bank for us on that. Just so you know, tricked out golf carts are not cheap.

So, in the short term, that solved the problem of making things right. Mr. Lawler's car was fixed and Jack had a new golf cart. Now, we just had to pay for it. Walt and I were both pretty relieved that we didn't have to worry about Jerry Lawler pinching our heads off. Jack was very pleased with his new golf cart. The new one had all the same stuff his old one had and more. Jack told us that he deserved an upgrade just because we had stolen and destroyed his old cart. This one had an eight-track tape player in the stereo, headlights that actually worked pretty well, and an ougah horn. This thing even had a windshield with a windshield wiper. Golf carts just don't get any fancier than that. Of course, Walt and I weren't allowed to touch it. Walt wasn't even allowed to look at it.

In the longer term, Walt and I had a problem. Between the two of us, we had to come up with about $150 every month to meet our obligations at the bank. That's a lot of money for a couple of high school kids who didn't have jobs.

In a month, Walt could earn his $75 easy working at his father's engineering firm. I had to find some sort of employment really fast.

At first, I got a job working nights at Minuteman Hamburgers. Because it was a food joint and paid restaurant minimum wage, I made seventy-five-cents an-hour. That meant that in a given month, just to make my $75 I had to work a hundred hours. That's twenty-five hours a week. I thought that sucked when I started, but I found out after two weeks that it really sucked super bad because the government takes a huge hunk of your money for taxes. If I worked one hundred hours, and put every cent toward my $75, I would still come up fourteen dollars short because the government take fourteen dollars out. This problem was short-lived because, as usual, things got worse. I pissed the manager off. I ended up getting fired. Just make a note, you just can't tell your boss that you have a dog smarter than him and expect to keep your job. It was, however, true.

I was in a jam. What I needed was a job where I couldn't get fired. I needed a job that I manage the time I worked so it didn't interfere with hunting. I needed a job that paid well enough that I could meet my obligations. I was really stuck. As each day crept by, I got closer to the end of the month when I was going to have to cough up $75 that I didn't have.

As the weekend approached, I had no job and no ideas. I was starting to panic. I was starting to wonder if The Goob, my little brother, had anything I could pawn.

Saturday morning, I was supposed to go duck hunting with Dad and a couple of his friends. I looked forward to this because it would give me a chance to think about something other than that damn $75. Dad ended up being on-call at the hospital, so he couldn't go on hunting on Saturday. I went his buddies anyway. The only reason I was invited to go in the first place was because I was the only one who could call ducks. All Dad's buddies were doctors. When they were in high school, instead of spending time learning how to call ducks, they spent their time learning chemistry and stuff like that. They couldn't call ducks for love or money. Everyone wanted to hunt with Dad because Dad would bring me. I didn't know diddly squat about chemistry but I sure as hell could call ducks. I could call ducks really well.

Dad's buddies and I went hunting. Once we got all situated in the blind, Dad's buddies, Dr. Manley and Dr. Blaine, wanted to know the whole scoop about the golf cart fiasco. They had heard about a dozen different versions of what happened. Seems that, in the short time since it had happened, the whole unfortunate incident had become something of a local legend. They wanted the true story. In between bringing flights of ducks into our decoys, I told them the whole story with some minor embellishments and a few strategic omissions. Dr. Manley was the orthopedic doc, who had told me my football days were over. After hearing the story, he commented that he didn't realize that football had been so important to me. I told him that I had been planning to be a professional football player my whole life. "Now," I said, "I got to figure something else out. It's a little late for that, don't you think?"

He smiled and looked at Dr. Blaine. Dr. Blaine had produced a flask and was taking a big pull on it. Finally, Dr. Manley said, 'Boy, I have seen you play." He accepted the flask from Dr. Blaine and continued, "You were never going to play pro football."

"You should become a doctor," Dr. Blaine chimed in. He took another big pull on the flask and handed it to Dr. Manley.

"Oh, now that's just kicking a man when he's down," I said as I scanned the sky for ducks.

Dr. Manley laughed and sputtered. I think he blew a little bourbon out his nose. Laughing, he nudged me. I looked at him and he passed me the flask. If Papaw wasn't around, I didn't often get offered bourbon. I figured I'd take advantage of the moment. I usually sip bourbon, but I took a big draw on the flask. I was used to drinking bourbon, but this wasn't bourbon. This was a Tennessee whiskey and it kind of took my breath for a second. I recovered pretty quickly when I spotted flying ducks in the distance. I blew a long, lonesome hail call and began to work a flight of about a dozen mallards flying about a quarter mile to the west of us over the L'Angiulle River. Between calls, Dr. Manley asked in a whisper how we were paying for Mr. Lawler's car repairs and Jack's new golf cart. I paused calling after the ducks had turned back toward us and gave up some altitude. You don't want to call too much. That's a mistake a lot of folks make.

I whispered that Walt was in good shape because he was making good money working at the engineering firm. Me, on the other hand, I was screwed. I told them that I had just got fired at the Minuteman Hamburgers, but I didn't tell them why. I was, I admitted, in a bit of a spot. The end of the month was coming and I was flat broke with no prospects for salvation. We all got low in the blind as the ducks, about twenty feet off the water, flew right over the blind. We could hear the low chatter they made, and the wind whistling on their wings as they passed. I hunkered down a little lower and answered them with a little chatter.

After the ducks passed us, I blew a real hard, sharp, hail call to bend them back to us. They turned back to us, and I shortened my call. They were coming into the wind with their wings cupped. They intended to light in among our decoys. I laid down a little more chatter as the came closer and closer. They were getting closer and lower heading for center of the decoys. Everybody hunkered down and got ready to shoot. I quit calling and whispered, "Wait till they are about a foot off the water and don't shoot my decoys!"

We all fired at the same time, and four of the twelve ducks fell from the sky. Dr. Blaine got one, as did Dr. Manley. I got two. Dr. Manly and Dr. Blaine both claimed my second duck. They argued good naturedly about it while I watched a headless decoy sink into the muddy water of the rice field.

As he looked out at the ducks lying among the decoys, Dr. Blaine smiled. He looked at me and said, "Boy, you ought to hire out as a professional duck caller." On hearing this, Dr. Manley seconded the motion. He looked at Dr. Blaine, then he and looked at me. Dr. Blaine grinned and took out a twenty-dollar bill. He said, "That's for today." He handed me a second twenty. "And that's for next Saturday," he added. Dr. Manley did the same. Between today's hunt and the hunt I booked for next week, I had the cash in my hand to pay my note and put some gas in my car. I was greatly relieved.

Dr. Manley told me to be sure and get twenty dollars from anyone else that they might bring next week. After the next week, word spread pretty fast and I booked every Saturday morning, and quite a few Saturday afternoons for hunting. If I hunted morning and evening, on a lot of those days, I was making more than a hundred dollars calling ducks. Sure beats the hell out of flipping burgers for seventy-five cents an hour.

I knew that duck season would eventually end so I figured I had to make hay while the sun shined. A tornado had blown the school away last May, so we went to school in portable buildings out at the fairgrounds. Everyone called it Heifer High. There was a space problem at the fairgrounds because there weren't enough temporary classrooms. People had different start times for their classes. Since my classes at school didn't begin until ten, I figured could hunt on some school days till about nine-fifteen, then haul ass to get to class on time. I started booking hunts on weekday mornings, too. This was working pretty well till I got busted in english class for forgetting to take my knife off of my belt.

My ten o'clock class was english. I was running late one morning and had to make a mad dash from the muddy pasture we called "a parking lot" to class. I was probably thirty seconds late when I entered the room. I didn't realize it, but Mrs. Smith, my English teacher, saw my knife on my belt as I slid into my desk. Mrs. Smith was a small, thin lady, who always looked like she was trying desperately to keep from farting. I saw her as she watched me run into the room and take my seat. She twitched a little and opened her eyes super wide. I thought she was just pissed because I was late again.

Mrs. Smith marched right over and laid a big-time evil eye on me. I don't think she liked me at all. She stood still as a statue right in front of my desk until I looked up at her. She held out her hand and sternly said, "I will have that knife." I didn't know what she was talking about at first because it had not occurred to me that my knife was still on my belt.

Startled, I said, "Ma'am?"

"That knife, young man. I will have that knife. Give it to me right now," she commanded. "And its little purse thing, too," she added referencing the knife case.

Almost as a reaction, I felt my belt, and sure enough, I found my knife. I knew I was in trouble. My heart sank. I knew the rule. I didn't have any problem with the rule. I didn't mean to break the rule, but there no way was I giving up my knife. This knife was special. It was a folding Buck knife with a five-and-a half-inch locking blade and walnut grips in a very rugged leather case. It was a hell of a fine pocketknife and this particular knife was really hard to get. If you could find another one, it would cost you ten dollars easy, maybe more.

"Mrs. Smith, I'm so sorry. I forgot to take the knife off my belt this morning. We were late getting in because we got the truck stuck…" I lied.

She cut me off. "Not another word. Give me that knife right now, or I will have Coach Harris handle this," she commanded. The whole room went absolutely silent at this point. No one moved. The room was absolutely silent and all eyes were on us. Mentioning Coach Harris was like threatening to bring the wrath of God down on someone. I hadn't meant to challenge her. I just wanted to go put my knife in the truck with my other hunting stuff. I knew if I gave her my knife, I would never see it again. I really didn't want to give up that knife. Her threat to send me to see Coach Harris hung in the room like the smoke from a cannon shot. Coach Harris was the principal of the high school. Most students feared that man more than death itself.

Seconds later, I left the portable building where class was and was walking to the administration building for a chat with Coach Harris. When I opted to go see Coach Harris rather than surrender my Buck knife, there was a rustling sound of people shifting uncomfortably in their chairs that went through the room. I heard it. I knew as I stood up to go to Coach Harris's office that everyone in the room thought that I was a dead man. To them, I know it must have seemed like Caesar had just crossed the Rubicon. The die was cast. The end was known. But no one knew that I knew something about Caesar that they didn't.

As I sat outside Coach Harris's office, I was wondering how bad this was going to be, but not for the reasons you might think. Roughly twenty years ago, Coach Harris was probably the finest athlete to ever come out of Sweetwater, Mississippi. Dad had been Coach Harris's family doctor in Sweetwater. Our families were such good friends that we stayed with his family for a few days after our house in Sweetwater burned down when I knocked the candle over... but that's another story.

I was just sitting there lost in thought. The door opened, and for a moment I thought it was Coach Harris. I was prepared for Coach Harris, but it wasn't him. It was Dezi, the little, short, blonde-headed girl who sat beside me in algebra. I have had something of a crush on her since fall, but I don't think I had ever spoken with her. I pretended not to notice as she walked to the desk in the corner.

"Are you here to see Coach Harris?" she inquired in a perky voice as she seated herself behind the desk.

"Yeah, Mrs. Smith wanted to confiscate my knife," I said as I looked up.

"Three days," she said casually, as she got comfortable at her desk and started tallying up the attendance reports.

"Three days? What about three days?" I countered.

"That what you'll get. A three-day suspension," she said with understated but knowing certainty.

"I doubt it," I replied, looking away.

Dezi, like everyone in my english class, only knew Coach Harris as principal of Jonbur High School. He was known to them as a man the devil himself would not tangle with. I knew him as a man who loved his steaks rare, his bourbon neat, and the hunting of all manner of critters.

Coach Harris left Sweetwater and came to Arkansas State College to play football. In coming to Arkansas State College, he set in motion the chain of events that culminated with our family moving from Sweetwater to Jonbur. Coach Harris, as you might have figured out by now, has known me my entire life. I knew that I could look forward to seeing him at dinner every New Year's Day. Dad, Coachie, and Coach Harris, would all watch football together all afternoon. I was pretty sure he wasn't going to give me licks with that paddle for forgetting to ditch the knife in my truck or suspend me, but I was worried that he might let the cat out of the bag to

Mom and Dad about my duck hunting enterprise. I was pretty sure Dad would not approve of this enterprise.

It wasn't real long before Coach Harris came striding into the room. When he entered a room, it was like he sucked all the oxygen out. He completely owned the room. You could just sense it. He was in charge. It was like someone turned on a heat lamp. You could just feel it.

He didn't even look at me as he walked past me and through the door to his office.

"Junior, get your ass in in here," he said in a low growl as he passed me. "And shut the door," he added with a voice that could have turned Satan into a pillar of salt. I knew this man as well as I knew anyone, and I understood that he had an image to maintain, but holy cow was I scared. Just his voice scared me. Smiling, Dezi teased me mouthing, 'Three days, Junior," to me as I rose to walk in the office.

I hated being called Junior.

By the time I got in the office, Coach Harris was sitting behind the desk in his office. The sun shining through the window directly behind him, Coach Harris looked like a god on a throne. He directed me to stand in squarely in front of the desk. His desk was clear of clutter and clean as a whistle. He carefully centered his hands on the calendar desk pad. I noticed that the calendar pad was absolutely clean. I had to squint from the glare of the sun through the window and I felt like I was at the Gates of Heaven about to be tested.

"What's all this crap I'm hearing about some damn knife?" he began as his eyes began to melt the flesh from my face.

One thing I absolutely knew about Coach Harris was that you get one chance to be truthful with him, and if you blow it, you are absolutely screwed. I set about explaining to him pretty much the whole story about my hunting operation, and how it was paying my loans for repairing Jerry Lawler's car and buying Jack's golf cart. He already knew all about the adventure on the golf course, but he hadn't heard the whole, true story. All he had heard was the gossip that went around town, so he wanted the inside scoop on that, too. He and Jack were good friends, too. He had actually ridden in the new golf cart, but he had not asked Jack about the events that produced the new cart. Jack, he knew, was still a bit touchy about it. As I told him the story, he smiled some, and at points laughed out loud. He was particularly interested in the part where Walt and I were trying to escape from the wreckage of the convertible top.

He really laughed hard about that and wanted to know about meeting Mr. Lawler. I saw very little humor in having a meeting with a man who makes his living throwing other men around a wrestling ring.

Finally, I told him about my duck hunting enterprise. I didn't go into a lot of detail because I really wanted to minimize the fact that I was making good money calling ducks.

Coach Harris stopped me. "So, let me make sure I understand this. You are working as an unlicensed duck hunting guide in the mornings before school."

I said, "Yes, sir. You could put it that way."

"And you are hunting four-to-five times a week," he continued.

"Counting weekends, yes, sir," I replied.

"And you are actually getting ducks?" Coach Harris inquired seriously.

"Oh yes, sir. We rotate our spots a lot but we limit out most every morning," I said with a nod.

Leaning in a little, Coach Harris inquired, "Junior, son, where are you hunting?"

I hesitated. Good hunting spots are gold. Finally, after considering the implications of this decision, I said, "Coach, I'll have to show you."

Coach Harris smiled and said, "Yes, I think you will."

Well, that solved that problem. I didn't have any more trouble out of Mrs. Smith, but I didn't abuse my privilege. When I ran late, I would always swing by the office, say "Hi" to Dezi, and pick up my get-out-of-jail-free card. I took great pains to not be late often. If your hunting buddy is the principal of the school, you can miss an astonishing number of classes and still not only show perfect attendance but also get an A for the semester. It didn't take algebra to figure out that in only thirty days of hunting, I could pay off the lion's share of my bank notes. Life was good as we got close to Christmas break at school.

In operating my hunting enterprise, I learned a lot about how to operate a business. I had learned that it was always a good idea to have some beer on hand and maybe a bottle or two of good wine. I found out early on that Boone's Farm is not considered good wine by most people. I made it my custom to always have a flask of bourbon on me. I mean real Kentucky Bourbon, not that crap from Tennessee. Usually I had a backup flask, too just in case because sometimes folks just needed more than just a sip or two to celebrate a good hunt. I lost a really good flask and learned not to offer Coach Harris a shot of morning bourbon before class. Things had certainly turned themselves around and life was good.

The first Saturday of Christmas break, my buddy, JD, and I went hunting. I really needed a break from hunting with Dad's buddies and from helping Mom get the house ready for Christmas. I had put up a million lights outside and helped decorate inside. Mom loved decorating and entertaining. At some point during the holidays, she always had a party or a tea or something. I didn't have to worry about that on this day. On this day, JD and I were headed into the Cache River bottoms for ducks. A cold front was supposed to come through later and bring some weather. That always pushed new ducks in. New ducks would not be gun shy at our hunting spots. We were all set to get a few of the new ducks.

JD and I loaded Duke and all our crap into the boat for the trip to the spot where we hunted. Duke was JD's dog. He's a black Lab and a fine dog to hunt with. When either of us downed a duck, Duke went out after the duck. Duke always enjoyed going after the ducks and it saved us a lot of work.

Our spot was about a thirty-minute boat ride through flooded woods. It was a pretty good ways through the flooded woods to get to the open channel. Once in the channel, we motored about another twenty minutes to our spot. We were pretty far out in the boonies. If you got in a jam out there, you were in a jam all by yourself. We put our decoys out where we always did and eased the boat back into the stand of flooded cane near the west bank of the slough.

It was while we were getting the boat situated that JD noticed that Duke was drinking something from the bottom of the boat. I looked, and damn if that dog wasn't drinking wine. Somehow the top on one of my wine bottles had come unscrewed and the wine was now in the bottom of the boat being drunk by Duke. Duke, it seems, likes wine a lot. JD, of course, thought this was hilarious. I didn't think it was very funny at all. Now I had to replace that bottle of wine before my next paying hunt.

While we were waiting for daylight, we talked a bit. Sometimes, when we were hunting, we talked about girls. I already had Dezi on the brain. Sometimes we talked about hunting and sometimes we talked about the best way to avoid the game wardens. I don't rightly remember if we talked much this day because just as soon as it was legal shooting time, ducks were all over us. We were having a good day calling and the ducks were working in close. On the first bunch, we shot and two ducks dropped into the water.

Usually just as soon as ducks started falling in the water, Duke would scramble out of the boat to go retrieve the ducks. On this day, Duke didn't move. JD looked at Duke. Then he looked at me with that "What in the hell" look on his face. JD hollered, "DUKE!" and pointed out where the ducks had fallen. Duke looked up over the gunwale of the boat for just a second, then lay his head back down. "DUKE!" JD sounded off again. Duke looked up at JD and growled.

Duke, it seems, was drunk, and we were learning that Duke is a mean drunk. For the next couple of hours, we tried to hunt. We'd call ducks in. They would work in really nicely. We'd shoot and get a couple. Duke would raise his head up and growl, but he would not go retrieve the ducks. We had to take the boat out of our hide, and motor around really carefully to get our ducks. On what turned out to be our final trip out to retrieve a duck, we got the prop of the boat fouled with the lines anchoring a couple of decoys. Duke was sleeping. It occurred to me that if Duke couldn't hold his liquor, he shouldn't drink so much. So as not to awaken the damn dog, JD and I both cussed Duke under our breath. We were in a jam.

Having the prop fouled meant that we couldn't use the motor. We could not get back to the truck without the motor. Both of us made a mental note that we ought to bring a paddle next time we hunt in the slough. We were in deep water, so walking around to the end of the boat to clear the prop was not an option. It was getting cold and the wind was coming up. We needed to clear the prop so we could motor our way out of the swamp before we started getting rain or sleet.

We lifted the prop out of the water, and JD tried to climb over the top of the motor to reach the prop, but that was no good. He almost fell in. It would not do to be wet when it is this cold. Finally, we had to remove the motor from the back of the boat and bring it in the boat with us so we could clear the prop. This was a one-person operation. JD got in the front of the boat, and I very carefully loosened the bolts and lifted the motor into the boat. Both of us knew that if I slipped and let the motor go, it would go right to the bottom of the slough and we would be stuck.

Well, the prop was a hell of a mess. There was about a mile of nylon string wrapped around the prop and we had to get all that off before we could use the motor. JD and I set to work. We took turns because it was cold, wet work and our fingers were getting cold and stiff. We took turns taking shots of bourbon from one of my flasks to stay warm. It helped some, but we were still freezing our asses off.

While we worked on getting the prop cleared, we talked some. I was still struggling some with what to do with my life. Just like everyone else, JD suggested I become a doctor. He didn't like my cowboy idea. No one seemed to understand how tough a life a doctor has. Everyone sees the big cars, but no one sees the pure bone-numbing exhaustion after a week of fourteen-hour days.

"Dad," I told JD, "always comes home dead tired, just worn out. He is just exhausted all the time. Mom is worried that one day he'll have a heart attack." I reflected for a minute on Dr. Sanders and his heart attack. I remembered when Dr. Sanders, Dad's favorite gastro guy, keeled over with a heart attack. I told JD about it. Dr. Sanders keeled over deader than a doorknob having coffee right there in the kitchen. We went over to visit Dr. Sander's wife that evening. There were about twenty cars parked all around the house. Dr. Sanders had done so many favors for so many people that everyone wanted to be there for Mrs. Sanders in her time of need.

JD suggested that I become some other kind of doctor, one that doesn't have to work so hard or have so much stress. "You know, you could be one of those zit doctors or an allergist," he said. "Their patients never die and they never get well," he added with an optimistic note.

We continued to make progress in clearing the prop, and the wind kept coming up more and more. It was a cold wind signaling that the cold front was arriving. Rain would start soon. It would be followed by sleet and maybe freezing rain. We needed to get the prop cleared and get out of the flooded woods. If we didn't hurry, we were going to get really cold, and really wet, really fast.

It took a while, but finally we got the last of the nylon string out of the prop and it was clear. As Duke slept peacefully in the bottom of the boat. Very carefully, we put the motor back on the back of the boat. We finished gathering up our decoys and set out to get back to the truck. JD was running the motor. We had a 9.8 horsepower Mercury motor on the back of a fourteen-foot aluminum jon boat. Usually we just putt-putt through the flooded woods being careful to avoid trees and stumps. But not this day. On this day, we were cold and we had been drinking bourbon for about an hour.

Flooded woods are just what it sounds like they are. The near constant rain of late fall has pushed the river out of its banks, and the woods lining the river are flooded. Out in the river channel, the water is deep. That's where we put decoys and hunted. In the flooded woods, it's not deep, maybe thigh deep. In the late spring when the water was down, it was there that we did some trapping. The trees are spaced out so that if you are just putt-putting along it's not a problem to weave your way through. You just motor along. If, however, you have been drinking bourbon all morning and have suddenly acquired supreme confidence in your boat handling skills, you will not putt-putt. You will fly. JD flew.

We were flying though the flooded woods like a greyhound on a rabbit's ass. I was very concerned about it. As we wove our way through the flooded woods, we kept brushing and bumping against trees. Sometimes it was just a light brush, and other times it was the "thud" of a brush. I hollered up to JD to slow down. All I got back was laughter so loud I could hear it over the motor. I made a mental note, "No more bourbon for JD."

We brushed a tree so hard that I nearly fell out of the boat. I hollered back to JD about it again. JD thought this was incredibly funny, flipped me the bird and opened the throttle up even more. We sped up even faster. That 9.8 Merc could really move a fourteen-foot jon boat. I felt like we were doing a slalom ski run down a snow-covered mountain the way we swooshed back and forth in and among the trees. Duke, was sliding from one side of the boat to the other as we shifted back and forth. I wondered how he could sleep through the impacts when we bounced off the trees. We were probably only a mile or so from the truck with only a couple more deep spots to clear when it happened.

We were going flat out thought the trees just as fast as a 9.8 horsepower Mercury outboard motor will run when JD misjudged the distance between two trees by just a smidgen. Sometimes a smidgen is all it takes to get a jon boat wedged between two trees. If you are going fast enough and the trees are close enough, you can wedge it so securely that the boat will go from a speed of about twenty-five-miles-per-hour to zero-miles-per-hour in the space of about four feet. That's exactly what we did. We went from twenty-five-miles-per-hour to zero in the space of about four feet.

When the boat got wedged it stopped, but we didn't. I was sitting in the front of the boat, so I flew out of the boat and skipped across the water like a fallen waterskier before finally sinking into the icy water. Duke, who had been quietly sleeping off all the wine he drank, slid violently forward, hit the metal front seat, got airborne and landed in the icy water. When he surfaced, Duke was really pissed.

JD was in the back of the boat. He hit the metal middle seat of the boat with both shins. This caused him to prone out some as he continued forward striking his head against the metal front bench of the boat before finally going airborne and landing in the water. JD came up much more sober, a little dazed and suffering from severe shin pain. I think the cold water is what sobered him up and kept him from being knocked unconscious.

I looked at the boat in amazement. The boat was wedged between two young pine oak trees that it had forced apart just a little. The trees were leaning apart sort of like a capital V. The boat was stuck in the "V" with the bottom of the boat suspended about eighteen-inches above the water.

As I said, when the boat stopped, we didn't. We all flew forward and into the water. All of our gear did the same. It was all in the water now. We had guns and ammo in the water. Guns and ammo, I might add, don't float. Decoys and empty beer cans, which do float, were everywhere. Cushions were floating nearby. It was a hell of a mess and a hell of a problem. Duke was really pissed now. He was mean drunk, but he was much meaner when he was woke up in the boat crash. He was chasing me and JD through the water intent on inflicting personal harm. While I was fleeing from Duke, I stepped in someone's trap which painfully caught my right foot. The trap was securely anchored, so now I was screwed. I could only run in a circle as Duke chased me. He got me a couple of times on the seat of my pants before JD got control of Duke and got him back in the boat.

With Duke back in the boat, JD gave him what was left of the wine to keep him pacified and occupied while we gathered up all our gear. It took some doing to find the guns because they sank into the muddy water. We were lucky the water was only about two feet deep. We were cold, and the wind was really blowing and it was starting to rain. This was getting serious, and we had to get the boat free so we could get back to the truck or we would soon freeze to death. JD mentioned that heart attacks are what kills most folks who die of hypothermia. Heart attacks! That's all I need to think about. What a cheery thought. JD had "heart attack" on the brain.

It took a supreme effort to get the boat free, but finally we did get it unstuck. I noticed right away that we had loosened some of the rivets, because my previously perfectly sound boat now leaked rather badly at several of the rivets. We maintained a much more reasonable rate of speed as we covered the last mile or so back to the truck. JD didn't do that because he had regained his right mind. He went slower because we were soaking wet and the cold wind made us even colder. We were both turning blue and shivering uncontrollably. This, I recalled from my hunter safety class, was stage two of hypothermia. It didn't take real long to get everything loaded in the truck. JD, Duke, and I, all piled into the front of the trunk for the short drive back to Jonbur. We were all chilled to the bone. JD and I had taken on a very blue complexion and were shivering uncontrollably. JD was shaking so bad he had a hard time getting the key in the truck. He fired up the truck and we headed home. We turned the heater on full blast. It didn't help right away because it takes a few minutes for the truck to warm up. We would probably be home before the truck heater got warm. Luckily, I had my backup flask. We began to draw off of it to try to speed our warming process. Duke didn't like bourbon, so it was just me and JD. I think Duke was still pretty buzzed from all the wine he had drunk.

When we rounded the corner in my neighborhood, my heart stopped. JD stomped the brake. In front of Mom and Dad's house there were cars everywhere.

"What in the hell?" I slurred.

"Holy shit!" JD shouted in a semi-drunk voice. "Your dad's had a heart attack!" He stomped the gas and popped the clutch. His Gumbo Mudder tires screamed as they laid down dark-black streaks on the gray asphalt pavement of Cardinal Road. We roared up the street like a comet. With the engine backfiring through the pipes, JD skidded sideways and very destructively through one of the gardens in our front yard, knocking over a bird bath and destroying a koi pond before coming to a very muddy stop near Mom's azaleas. Still dripping wet, covered in mud and with all of my duck hunting gear hanging off of me, I sprinted toward the house followed closely by JD and Duke. I almost knocked the wreath right off the front door as I ran in the house. I stopped dead in my tracks. JD and Duke, following closely, each slammed into me, one at a time, each knocking me just a step or two deeper into the room. All three of us froze at the sight before us.

We were greeted by what appeared to be the entire membership of St. Elmo's Episcopal Church, all nicely attired in their holiday best and lined up at a beautiful buffet. Mom, Dad, Sweet Pea, and the Goob, were all standing up front beside Father Patrick, our new Episcopal priest. It appears they were about to say the blessing. Mom was dressed in a beautiful holiday dress with a very complementary shawl. Dad was in his standard Brooks Brothers suit. Sweet Pea looked like a Vogue cover model. The Goob wore gray pants, a blue button-down shirt with a cardigan sweater. His hair was neatly combed. All stood together at the head of the room. The entire room was frozen as if in a mosaic. Every single person was looking silently looking at JD, Duke, and me. Not a sound, save for the water dripping from us, could be heard in the room. Mom went a little pale, started to wobble a bit. Then she put her face in her hands. Sweet Pea had her eyes wide open and her hand covering her mouth. The Goob just blinked. He didn't move a muscle. He just blinked. Dad stood there with absolutely no expression whatsoever. The whole room was absolutely silent and motionless.

JD, Duke, and I, stood there taking all this in. We were still shivering and our complexions were still pretty blue from hypothermia. We were covered in mud, reeking of bourbon, and dripping muddy water on the antique Persian rug that protected Mom's beautiful hardwood floor. I had a duck call around my neck and a buck knife on my belt. My faded jeans were covered in mud and had a tear and a little blood on the seat of my britches where I had suffered a near miss from Duke. Duke broke wind and gave a good shake, releasing a mist of water that silently expanded throughout the room.

It occurred to me that there may have been a misunderstanding about the date of the tea party.

Dad straightened his tie a little and adjusted his posture. Recovering his composure and staring straight at me, with the measured dignity of a master diplomat he said, "And this," he paused and took a deep and reluctant breath, "is my other son."

Mom fainted.

A Water Hazard

Dad and I had a long talk about growing up, about responsibility and about dignity. Being responsible and developing some dignity is very important for a young man. It was in high school, he said, that folks need to start thinking about their future and shaping their conduct and actions in ways that develop responsibility and dignity. Doing that will help lead to the future a person seeks.

"We," he said, "control our own destiny." He looked at me with knowing eyes and said, "As we grow into adults, we must mold ourselves in accordance with social rules and norms that enable us to grow into good men." He had placed emphasis on "good" and he paused for just a second to see if I understood. I nodded knowingly but was, in reality, somewhat lost. Was he saying that I was not a good guy? I was trying to be a good guy, but things just seem to happen.

Looking off, as if into the clouds, he finished, "We reinforce not only the good image that others see of us, but we also fortify our self-image with strength that we can draw on in difficult times. Remember, we help those who cannot help themselves, and we defend those who cannot defend themselves. We are gentlemen at all times." He said it might be a good idea if I kept that in mind and worked toward that end.

I nodded again, and said, "Yes, sir."

"Crap, that's a damn tall order," I thought to myself. Now, a little while ago I was questioning my fitness to become a doctor. Now, I was questioning my fitness in general.

I decided to talk to my sister, Sweet Pea, about this. She generally had good advice about all kinds of things. Sweet Pea has always said life is all about choices. "You have choices at every juncture in life," she began, "and outcomes are pretty much dependent on whether or not you have good luck." That seemed to make pretty good sense to me. Good luck is a pretty important thing to have.

"Having good luck is so important, that you just cannot leave having it to chance," she said as she dug in her purse to find something. Having found what she was looking for, she continued, "See this?" She held up a dead mouse. "I have good luck," she said, "because I bought it when we lived in Memphis."

I looked closely at the lump of fur in her hand. "You bought that? It looks like a stuffed mouse," I said not quite following what she meant.

"It was a mouse, but now it's a talisman. When we lived in Memphis, I went down to Voodoo Village. I gave a witch doctor twenty dollars to give me a good luck talisman."

She held up the dead mouse.

"A witch doctor gave you a dead mouse for twenty bucks?" I said.

"It just looks like a mouse because it was a mouse. Now, it's a talisman," she said. "I carry it everywhere. And ever since I got it, I've had good luck with everything, even math."

I paused and thought for a minute. Sweet Pea didn't need good luck with math. That really was her superpower. This wasn't making much sense.

"You said you had a talisman. That's a dead mouse. You carry a dead mouse everywhere?" I said still not quite believing what I was hearing.

"The mouse is the talisman," she replied somewhat impatiently, "and I carry it everywhere because you can never tell when you might need some good luck."

"How can you tell when it's working?" I asked.

Sweet Pea looked at me like I had two heads. "You know it's working because you have good luck," she finally said.

According to her, because I didn't have good luck because either because I was born naturally unlucky (in which case I was screwed and nothing will help) or because someone had put a curse on me. It had to be one or the other. It might be that I was born unlucky she said because I had knocked over the candle that burned the house down. I pointed out to her that was a result of a sneeze, so it was probably allergies and not bad luck. That being the case, she suggested that I get religion.

"You should probably stick to Christian religions. If you haven't already sinned your way into hell," she said, "getting on the right side of the Good Lord might be your only hope."

"Depending on how you categorize the various sins, I might be cutting that pretty close," I thought. I told her that I'd give it some thought.

I wanted to talk to The Goob about it, but he wouldn't talk to me. He said Sweet Pea told him I had bad ju-ju. He wanted to be careful so that I didn't give it to him. I wasn't aware that bad luck was contagious, but I understood.

Mom had a relapse of her nerves right after the tea party. A lot of folks think it was because of my entrance at the tea party, and I kind of think that might be right. She was having a really tough time. She just seemed like she was on edge all the time. Dr. Weisseman gave her some pills that she was supposed to take whenever she felt the nervousness coming on. Father Patrick gave her a prayer to pray when she felt it coming on. Dad asked me to stay away from Mom as much as possible. I really felt badly, and I set out to try to be a better son.

I tried to get religion for a while, but it wasn't catching for me. To be honest, I really didn't try very hard. I decided to go another way. Religion seemed like a pretty significant commitment, and I just wasn't ready for that. It seemed to me if I stayed away from places where trouble was likely to find me, trouble was not likely to come looking for me. I figured that I might be able to avoid trouble for a while if I just stayed in the house. It was dead of winter, and duck season was over. I had paid off my bank notes. There wasn't anything to do anyway, so I focused on studying. I figured I'd start doing the sorts of things Mom and Dad enjoyed doing. They never seemed to have the sorts of problems that I did, so I figured it would be safe to give that a shot.

Mom and Dad both enjoyed the Country Club. Dad played golf and Mom socialized. I figured that I would start playing golf again. Dad had taught me to golf when I was really small and I used to play a lot. I had gotten away from golf when I started hunting and fishing. With spring coming soon, it would be time for golf in no time. Dad and I talked golf, and he was glad I was going to play more. The fact that there is no trouble to get in while playing golf at the golf course had not escaped me.

Even though it was still kind of cold, I started practicing golf. When you play golf, you have to dress sort of nice, in a country club kind of way. You wear stuff at the Country Club that no one would ever wear anywhere else. I'm not sure why the Club had its own rules as to fashion, but it did. Best I could figure out was that as long as it was bright colors and made out of double-knit polyester, you were good. So most days, after school, I dressed up like I was supposed to and went to work on my golf game. Mom and Dad both seemed really happy about it. Mom was really working on getting her nervousness under control and it really showed. Her eye hardly twitched at all anymore. I thought, "This is turning out okay."

While I was on the practice tee hitting balls, I spent a lot of time thinking about Dezi. Even though I sat beside her in algebra, we didn't really talk much. When we did speak, she always wanted to know what I said to Coach Harris that day I got sent to his office. She really wanted to know not only how I avoided a three-day suspension, but also how I scored all those get-out-of-jail-free cards when I was late.

"There's something fishy going on here," she used to say. I wouldn't tell her because you can't have something like that getting out. She really wanted to know.

Sometimes we talked about algebra. I had wanted to ask her out for a long time, but it never seemed to work out. I wanted to ask her out back in the fall, but I hesitated. That was probably a good thing because I found out she had a crush on Chet. Chet was tall and handsome. He had long, dark hair and Elvis-style sideburns. When she finally got over him, I wanted to ask her to the Christmas ball, but I hesitated again. Tox asked her first so I had to wait for her to get over him. Tox had a Paul McCartney look about him. Tox was a great guy. He was smart and had a great sense of humor, so it took a while for her to get over him. Now it was spring, and I was determined to take her out.

In late February of 1974, a new southern rock band was emerging. They were like the Allman Brothers, but different. They were on a nationwide tour of tiny venues when their album leaped onto the charts. Overnight, they became rock stars. They were booked into The Strand Theater for a concert in March. I quickly acquired a ticket to the show.

Somehow our very first non-algebra conversation centered on this concert. It came very close to being a giant disaster, but I don't think she ever knew. It was in the course of that conversation that I managed to invite her on a date to a concert for which I had only one ticket. Who in the hell does that? What in the hell happens in your brain for something like that to happen? Lynyrd Skynyrd had become an overnight success, and they were booked to play a concert in the old Strand Theater in Jonbur. There were only a thousand tickets and I had one, only one. Not two, but one. I had one ticket and I had just invited this beautiful, sweet girl with blue, blue eyes to go with me to the concert. I had one damn ticket. What the hell was I thinking? This was the first time that I became aware that my brain stopped working when I was talking to a pretty girl. (This seems to be a pattern in my life.) Right now, my problem was how to come up with second ticket to the sold-out Lynyrd Skynyrd concert.

As I said before, Skynyrd had only recently exploded onto the music scene. The only reason they were even playing in Jonbur was because the date was booked before their album became a monster hit. If they all hadn't been good ole boys, I think the band would have broke the contract, booked into the Mid-South Coliseum and made a hell of a lot more money. Ticket demand was so great in Jonbur that I knew beyond a shadow of a doubt that a ticket could not be had at any price. I was in a jam.

Even though it was late February, it was kind of a springtime cold. As had become my custom when confronted with a problem, I walked out to one of the ponds on the Country Club course. There, I quietly sipped bourbon from my flask and watched the ducks paddle about while I thought the problem through. I just couldn't understand how I managed to get in this jam. It wasn't like I didn't know I only had one ticket, or that I didn't know it would be impossible to get another one. What was I thinking? Did I think a second ticket would materialize out of thin air?

Bourbon is a great drink for contemplating things. It is the rich, interesting and very wise uncle of whisky. It is meant to be enjoyed with a good cigar, deep thoughts, and interesting company. Whisky is Irish for "water of life," and let me tell you, that is exactly what it is. Bourbon is aged in oak barrels and takes on a ton of interesting flavors. You don't drink this stuff in a gulp like they do in westerns on TV. What they drink on TV is whisky from Tennessee. Bourbon is to be sipped, savored, contemplated, understood, and appreciated. There are a lot of different flavors tucked into those tiny sips and the key is to always take tiny sips. I usually take about a thimble full, and let it find all parts of my mouth. It's a casual thing that promotes clear thinking. It is truly the elixir of the gods. If Papaw didn't teach me anything else, he did teach me to appreciate good bourbon.

I was sitting on the patio by the big pond up by the club house watching folks play the 18th hole. I was very discrete when I'd take a sip. I wished I had a good cigar. Just when I was about to lose hope and concede that there was no reasonable way to resolve my problem, I had stroke of inspiration. It came to me right out of the clear blue sky. I had taken my ticket with me to the pond. I pulled it from my pocket and looked at it closely. General Seating! It said "General Seating!" I examined it even closer and it was printed as cheaply as I remembered. It was just a very cheaply printed ticket on white card stock! It was all black ink and plain nondescript lettering. Nothing fancy at all! I looked closely at it again, examining every aspect. There were no graphics or nothing, just a plain black-and-white ticket. It was a ticket I was certain that I could duplicate using a felt tip pen and a white index card. I love moments like this. Just when all seemed lost, out of nowhere a great idea emerges! The trumpets blast, the angels sing, and there is salvation!

I had ten days to create a perfect replica of my ticket, plenty of time. I didn't want to call it what it was. Replica sounded better than "fake." The word "replica" didn't sound illegal. "Fake" was almost as bad as "counterfeit." Both of them sounded like a crime.

Using a straight edge, a very sharp felt tip pen, and an enormous number of plain, white index cards I went to work. I found that it was surprisingly difficult to create a fairly reasonable and convincing facsimile of the original ticket. Printed text is surprisingly difficult to accurately recreate with a felt tipped pen. Finally, after uncounted efforts using all the skills I had learned in art class, I produced a replica ticket that looked pretty good. I held it up and looked at it. I compared it to the original. I was pleased, but then I noticed that something wasn't quite right. The thickness of the index card stock was just a little off. I figured it would be good enough so that if you didn't have a real ticket in your hand to compare to, it would probably be okay.

The day of the concert arrived. I arrived at Dezi's house about fifteen minutes early. I didn't want to be late, so I got there early. I had only been in the driveway for about five minutes or so when Dezi's father looked out the window. I smiled and waved at him and he waved back. He didn't smile. In just a minute or two he came out to see if I was okay. I told him everything was fine and explained I had a date with Dezi, and that I got there early because I didn't want to take any chances about being late. He gave me a weird look and asked me to come on inside.

Dezi's mother laughed when we entered, and he told her why I was in the driveway. Dezi's mother, Oleane, was super nice, told me I needed a haircut and gave me a glass of tea. I sat down in a really cool green chair over by the ping pong table in the recreation room to wait on Dezi. The chair swiveled and rocked back some. It was a cool chair. I talked with her little brother while I waited. He was about four or five years old, and he was a very busy little boy. He was a body in constant motion climbing under the pool table, then over the foot stools, over the back of a chair and then up and down the step in the room. He was making me tired just watching him. It wasn't too long when Dezi came out and we left for the concert.

The concert was at The Strand. It was an old movie theater. Years and years ago, it had been a vaudeville theater, so it had a stage, tall curtains, and dressing rooms and stuff. After that, it was converted to a movie theater and that's where we went to see movies on Saturday when we were kids. It still showed movies for the most part now, but they had it fixed so they could do shows also.

Dezi and I parked a couple of blocks away and walked to The Strand. The line was already around the corner. We stood in the long, cold line outside The Strand. We shivered in the night air. It was early March, after all. I gave Dezi the real ticket and I planned on using the replica. It was a long line. We stood there shivering for what seemed to be hours before they finally opened the doors and began taking tickets up. It was a simple arrangement. They had one of the front doors open, and a guy at a card table taking up tickets by tearing them in half. He kept one half and gave the other half back to you.

With each step closer to the ticket taker, my confidence in my replica ticket receded. I grew less and less certain of my prospects for successfully gaining entry to the concert. I looked at the replica in my hand, and somehow now, standing in line, it appeared much less convincing than it had appeared at my desk at home. Though reasonably similar at home, the difference in the card stock of the original ticket from the card stock from the replica ticket was now glaringly apparent to my hand. At home, they felt nearly the same, but here, as we stood six people in line from the ticket taker, there was a clear, obvious and unmistakable difference. My ticket was no longer an outstanding replica. It was a lousy fake, a counterfeit, and I was pretty sure that they put counterfeiters in jail. Having already experienced one visit to the jail by virtue of my science fair project last year, I was quite certain

I did not want to go there again. I was quite certain that I would not do well in jail. Despite it being a cold March night, I was now sweating, sweating like mad.

When we were only two people away from the ticket taker, I was getting lightheaded. I had to fight to prevent hyperventilation. Dezi was trying to carry on a conversation of sorts, but I was trying to conceal my absolute panic from her. She must have thought I was having a nervous breakdown. I was sweating profusely. There just is no way to conceal the absolute terror I was experiencing. In mere moments, I was certain that I was going to be tackled by huge cops and dragged away, kicking and screaming, to jail for using a counterfeit Lynyrd Skynyrd ticket.

We stepped up to the ticket taker. My heart was racing so that I thought it might burst from my chest. My head was spinning. I was breathing as if there was not enough air on the earth, and sweat was rolling down my face. Dezi smiled and handed her ticket to the ticket taker. I heard it as he tore the ticket in half. The sound of the tearing of the ticket was, for that moment, the only sound that cut through the low murmur of the conversations going on, at the moment, all around me. The tearing sound was crystal clear. It seemed to echo in my brain. He gave Dezi one half of the ticket and she waltzed into the lobby of The Strand. It was now my turn. As

I handed my fake ticket to the guy taking tickets at the desk, I was more than a little nauseous. I noticed my hand shook as if I had suddenly developed a bad case of Parkinson's disease. With one eye twitching like hell, I forced myself to smile and look at the ticket taker.

Holy cow! I knew this guy. He was an older guy I knew from swim team, and he was as stoned as it is humanly possible to be.

He took my ticket. He didn't even glance up as he tore it in half and gave me my half. I entered into Valhalla.

Dezi and I found seats in the balcony near the fire escape. (You should always sit near the fire escape in a theater.) Sitting there waiting for the band to start, I reflected on what I had just done. It was not lost on me that I was now a criminal. I considered the implications of a criminal lifestyle. I began to silently repent my criminal ways. I solemnly resolved then and there to abandon my life of crime and return to the straight and narrow. Just then, someone nudged me. My heart stopped. I looked over expecting to see the long arm of the law there to drag me out of The Strand, but I was pleasantly surprised to find a grinning friend passing me an illegal smile. I paused momentarily, briefly and quickly reconsidering on my recent and most heartfelt repentance of the criminal life.

Well, that was our first date. The concert was great and I don't think Dezi ever found out that I made a fake ticket to get in. We started dating fairly steady. We went to see every movie that came out that spring. *Great Gatsby* was probably my favorite, but I think Dezi liked *The Sting* better. Mom and Dad seemed pretty happy with things because they really liked Dezi and I hadn't been in any trouble at all in well over a month. My grades in algebra and chemistry were up and my scores in golf were down.

Life was indeed good when I asked Dezi to play in the Memorial Day Golf Tournament with me. It was a tournament for couples. Though I had never played in it, I had always heard that it was always a lot of fun. It was one of those tournaments where it was actually more important to look good than it was to play good. The *Ladies of the Club* was an informal woman's group at the club. They always ensured that a bar was set up on the patio near the 18th green so folks could enjoy a cocktails and snacks as they watched the golfers play the 18th hole. The *Ladies of the Club* organized everything and it was all very elegant and very special. I was a little nervous, though because this was the first big event I had been to at the Club since Walt and I destroyed Jack's golf cart. I was sure there would be whispers and questions. Dezi and I weren't going to use a golf cart. We were planning on walking the course.

I woke early on the day of the tournament. I ate breakfast, showered, and dressed, before I drove over to Dezi's house in my freshly cleaned Caddy. The Caddy, you might recall, was a gift I received from Elvis after he, The Goob, and I, recaptured that big bastard at Graceland when I was a kid. Mom had used it for the most part since I got it. It was about seven or eight years old and showed its age. Dezi came out of the back door of her house and took my breath away. She wore white shorts, a white knit top, and had a white visor and golf glove. She looked like a commercial for a shampoo or something. The light spring breeze blew her long, blonde hair ever so slightly and I fought to keep from hyperventilating. Already I was having trouble thinking of what to say. Brain lock was striking again. I managed to put her clubs in the back of the car without getting grease on either them or me. We drove to the Country Club.

At the Club, the match began pretty much the way all golf matches start. Each foursome takes it's turn at the tee and begins the long journey through eighteen holes. We were way back in the order, so we had plenty of time to enjoy a cup of coffee and a donut or two. You need to be relaxed to play golf.

When you are playing golf you spend a lot of time walking to your ball. Dezi and I had a great time visiting while we walked. I enjoyed telling her about The Goob, and when he tried to fly when he was about three. She got a good laugh out of that, but I'm not sure she believed me when I said that I had tried to tell him that he couldn't fly. There was just a look in here eye that told me she wasn't buying it. It is true, however. I did tell him he couldn't fly. Of course, when he wouldn't listen and kept insisting that he could fly, I got frustrated and told him to prove it. Dezi didn't need to know that part.

She was amazed when I told her about Sweet Pea's dead mouse. One time, I told her, when Sweet Pea and I were supposed to be taking care of The Goob while Mom and Dad went to a medical meeting in San Francisco, Sweet Pea lost her mouse. Sweet Pea was going nuts looking for it. We found Miss Lady, Mom's little poodle, dead with the mouse right beside her. It looked like Miss Lady had tried to eat the mouse and then puked it back up. Sweet Pea was in a panic. I told Sweet Pea that if the damn mouse was really magic, that Miss Lady would come back to life. Sweet Pea just scowled at me, and said the mouse wasn't a magic mouse, that he was a talisman. I'm still not sure exactly what a talisman is, but I do know what a dead dog is. Eventually, we went all over town looking for another dog that looked like Miss Lady. We finally found one at Dr. Cairo's animal adoption place. Mom thought something was wrong with Miss Lady when she got home she wasn't acting right. She wouldn't come when you called her name, she loved to be petted and she didn't growl or bite anyone at all. We told Mom that Miss Lady just missed her a lot while she was gone and had just changed her ways.

Actually, the dog we got her was a lot nicer and easier to get along with than Miss Lady ever was. Sweet Pea washed off her dead mouse and put it back in her purse. Dezi commented that I came from a strange family. I wasn't quite sure how to take that.

With conversation like that, it's no wonder that the round of golf seemed to fly by. I wasn't playing badly and neither was Dezi. We weren't going to win any prizes, but we had a really good time and we looked great. From tee to green, we walked and talked together. She helped me strategize my shots, estimate the distances, and pick my clubs. I did the same for her. As we approached the 18th tee, I remember thinking that this may be the very best day of my life. One more hole, and then we would finish the day at the post tournament party, enjoy a wonderful dinner and dance the night away.

The 18th hole at the Country Club was a par four that had a tiny creek, a minor water hazard, cutting across the fairway about two-thirds of the way down the fairway. Even though there was a bridge over the creek on the left-hand side of the fairway, in most places the creek was so small that, if you had long legs, you could probably just hop over it. The green was right up by the club house. There were a number of huge, old oak trees between the club house and the green. They set up some tables and chairs as well as a bar on the patio in the shade of the old live oak trees so people could watch foursomes finish their round. Cocktails were abundant. The crowd enjoys casual conversations and cocktails, while watching the foursomes dressed in all their spring finery, finish their round.

My tee shot was good and just cleared the creek on the left-hand side of the fairway, just beyond the little bridge. Dezi's drive came up short of the stream on the right side of the fairway. We walked together most of the way, and then she went to the right to get to her ball. She knew what club she wanted, so she took her 4 iron with her. I pulled her cart with me. I crossed the creek on the little bridge on the far left of the fairway and walked up toward my ball.

Dezi reached her ball and prepared to hit. I stopped and watched. Holy cow, she was beautiful. She had perfect posture as she settled into her stance. I forgot to breathe. She would look down intently at the ball, and then back up at the green where she wanted to hit the ball. She made a few adjustments to her stance and looked again. Satisfied, I saw her deliberately relax her body, and the begin a smooth and graceful backswing. She paused just for a fraction of a second at the top of her swing, and then she swung through the ball. It took off on a high arch toward the green. I could tell she was going to be a little short, but it might make the green on the roll. In the distance, you could hear light applause and polite murmurers of approval from the small crowd watching from the patio by the green. Dezi looked up and smiled. She was pleased with the shot.

I began my pre-shot ritual. I selected my club and began working my feet to get lined up properly. I looked over at Dezi. The spot on the creek where Dezi stood spanned perhaps two feet of trickling water. Just from her posture, I could see what she was thinking. Dezi backed up a few steps and got a running start. Expecting to land lightly on the turf on the other side of the creek, she easily and gracefully cleared the creek with an effortless leap. She was, after all, a gymnast. Unfortunately, the turf on other side of the creek was not solid, not solid at all. It was more like turf resting on brown, chocolate quicksand. Even though she landed as gentle as an angel alighting on a cupcake, her right foot immediately sank almost up to her knee in the thick brown muck. I couldn't believe what had just happened. She had nailed the one-footed landing in the mud and sunk up to her knee. Now she was standing, looking a little silly, with one leg knee-deep in the mud, and the other high and dry hovering above the turf. It made her look like a three-and-a-half-foot-tall, ice-skating trophy. I looked up the fairway at the green. A couple of people on the patio had heard her call to me. They turned and were watching us.

Dezi had one of those "Oh my God" looks on her face. I didn't know whether to laugh or what. With her golf club in one hand and balancing on the one foot stuck in the mud and the other foot held just above the mud, she was stuck in an odd pose.

Without taking my shot, I left our clubs right where they lay and trotted over to her. Helping Dezi out of the mud took precedence over making a shot. I laughed a little. You have to admit that this was a little funny. I wished I had a camera. What a shot for the yearbook!

"Help me out of here," Dezi pleaded as she struggled to maintain her balance in that awkward stance. Again, I glanced down the fairway at the 18th green. More people were gathering to watch from the patio. Some were using the binoculars that had been placed on the tables so folks could identify distant players.

"Just hang on, I'll help you out," I said. I carefully eased as far onto the soft turf as I dared. The brown mud oozed up the sides of my shiny, new golf shoes. The ground beneath my feet was very questionable. I didn't want to join her in the quicksand mud trap, but I had to get closer if I was going to help her. The turf was very spongy beneath my feet. I looked down at my golf shoes. They were already completely covered in mud. The new white laces were already brown. Despite the cleats on my golf shoes, I thought my feet might slip out from underneath me at any moment. Dezi was valiantly trying to maintain her balance on one foot in the mud. She was beginning to tire in that awkward pose. She had set her club down in the mud so she could put that hand down to steady herself a little.

"I've got to get out of this! I'm getting a cramp. I can't stand like this much longer!" Dezi pleaded.

As I drew near to her it became clear that I could not reach her with my outstretched hand. She picked the club up, and she reached out to me with it. The club was covered in slick brown mud. She put her second foot down lightly in the muck, about a foot and a half in front of the stuck foot. It sank in the mud up to her ankle. She was just short of reaching me with the club, so I ventured a little closer and reached again. I sank up to my ankle. Her forward foot sank deeper into the muck with each movement she made. It seems quicksand mud was meeting all the expectations I had developed watching Tarzan movies as a kid. I was determined that I was not going to lose her to the muck. Both of my feet were in the mud up to my ankles now. I crept yet closer and until finally I was able to grasp the slippery, muddy grip of the club. I offered resistance as she tried to extract her foot from the mud. No good. And worse, now when she attempted to pull her stuck leg out, her foot was trying to slip out of her shoe. We regrouped and tried again. I noticed that everyone on the patio at the 18th green was watching us now.

"Try pulling it up slower," I urged. This only resulted in a gurgling sound as her foot came out of her shoe more slowly.

"It sounds like something is drowning," Dezi observed.

"Something is drowning," I said. "Us."

We tried again. As I pulled harder, she strained to extract her foot from the mud. The mud was making kind of a slurping sound as her foot slowly began an escape. Suddenly the turf beneath my feet gave way. My feet flew out from under me as if I was on ice. As I slipped, Dezi's muddy hands lost her grip on the muddy golf club. The club, freed from Dezi's hand, struck me right between the eyes, opening a pretty good cut just above my nose and causing a gushing nosebleed. Dezi, losing all resistance, lost her balance and fell backwards into the mud. We both landed flat on our back, sort of like when you make a snow angel, in a sea of liquid brown mud. Extracting Dezi from the mud had turned into quite the wrestling match. Again, as she sat up in the mud, the freeing of her upper body from the mud caused a loud slurping sound. The deep and soft mud captured my legs as I struggled to help her up. Her foot was still stuck in the muck. Frustrated, I grabbed her under the arms and lifted. When she finally came free, it was, of course, sans shoe. Each step we took to escape the mud resulted in yet another plunge into the mud. Finally, after a titanic struggle, we escaped the grip of the quicksand mud and made it to solid ground. Safe at last, or so I thought.

As we lay breathing heavily in the fairway, Dezi reminded me that she had lost a shoe. Between Walt and Dezi, shoes were going to be the death of me. Already exhausted, I reluctantly returned to the mud pit to retrieve Dezi's golf shoe. On my hands and knees, I reentered the mud. I began reaching down into the muck exploring the deep footprints for the missing shoe. After failing to find the shoe a couple of times, I finally came up with her shoe. We were completely covered from head-to-toe in mud and blood. You could not tell what the original color of our clothes had been, and our faces and hair were dripping mud. We looked as if we had been dipped in chocolate and rolled in straw. The crowd at the 18th green stood motionless in stunned silence.

I retrieved the golf bags, and we slowly began the long walk up the fairway to the green and the cocktail party.

Just then Mom, with a gleaming smile, sporting a light tan, dressed in a beautiful white sundress and Jackie-O sunglasses, breezed onto the patio at the 18th green to begin her shift as Hostess of the Green. Being Hostess of the Green was an honor shared among the women who organized the cocktail party on the patio near the 18th green. Mom noticed everyone was looking intently at the golfers walking up the fairway.

Mom casually picked up a pair of binoculars and peered down the fairway.

Marooned

A lot of folks have said they can imagine how much trouble all that caused. Let me assure you that they were wrong. It was an order of magnitude worse than anyone could imagine. No one could possibly anticipate the catastrophic results of that particular adventure. Mom had a major relapse. It was so bad that Dad suggested that I spend the summer working at the farm. He wanted me out of the door by five each morning so that mom could rest as long as she wanted. He asked me not to come home till after Mom went to bed. My beautiful Caddy was, of course, bathed in mud from the drive home. Cleaning it was a nightmare. The Country Club fined Dad for the damage we did to the fairway, and I was banned from the Club once again. The good news is that they didn't kick Dad out this time. Dezi wouldn't take my phone calls. Since school was out, I didn't get to see her every day. Working at the farm where I didn't have access to a phone, I didn't get to call except at lunch when I was at the Dawson's store. Even when I did call, there was no answer.

Like most times when I was in a jam, I turned to Sweet Pea for advice. She was usually pretty good with coming up with a solution to whatever problem I had. Usually, I had math problems. As I have said before, math was her superpower. I was okay with working on the farm all summer because I planned on being a cowboy anyway. Dezi not speaking, however, to me was a tough pill to swallow. I figured that if Sweet Pea could figure out all this algebra stuff, figuring out how to get Dezi to speak to me would be a snap.

Well, I was wrong. When I approached Sweet Pea for advice, she already knew what I was going to ask. She barely looked up from writing in her notebook. Before I could say anything, she said, "You should have got religion."

"I tried to," I lied, knowing in my heart that I hadn't made much of an effort. "I just couldn't find it. What's your mouse think?"

"Don't be stupid," she said, looking at me very condescendingly before she turned her focus back to her trigonometry. "He doesn't think anything. He is a talisman not an oracle."

"An oracle?" I wondered. By now, I was pretty sure a talisman was a breed of mouse, but what in the hell was an oracle? Why in the hell couldn't she just speak English? With that final comment, she went back to doing her trigonometry and ignored me. I wondered two things. One, why Sweet Pea was doing trigonometry in the summer? And two, was it too late to swing a deal with Jesus?

The Goob, of course, wasn't speaking to me because Sweet Pea had warned him that I had bad juju. I called him from a pay phone and convinced him that bad juju couldn't jump over a phone line. He wasn't much help, though. He was too busy to think about it much. Last year, I showed him three chords on the guitar. Now he has a band and they are going on tour to support the album they recorded.

So, at this point, it would be fair to say that my life really sucked and most folks are probably thinking this can't get any worse. Well, all, y'all are wrong.

As I mentioned before, It was now summer and Dad wanted me out of the house every day before Mom got up in the morning so that I didn't run the risk of upsetting her. On about the fourth or fifth day of working on the farm, I got up, fixed a cup of coffee. I got in the truck and took off for the farm at about five that morning. It's a very hilly and curvy fifteen miles out to the farm. Twelve miles are on an old highway, and three miles are on gravel. It can be a very leisurely, relaxing drive. You can get some good thinking done on a drive like that. On this morning, I was in no particular hurry. I was bummed out because of the mess I had caused. I was just jamming a little to the music on my AM radio, enjoying a good, hot cup of coffee, breathing the cool, early morning air and cruising out to the farm for what I expected to be a long day on horseback. There were fences to be checked. The hills and curves made for a fun, slow drive, but the drive is more fun if you go a little faster. I sped up.

My headlights combined with the early morning light made the sights in the trees that hug the highway interesting. Some folks would tell you that they've seen Bigfoot in those woods. I think they saw a mangled tree trunk as their headlights swept the tree line. With a little more speed, the mailboxes began to flash by in the headlights like an almost lost memory of last night's dream. In the curves and cresting the hills, the headlights scan the woods in a blur as the truck, tires squealing just a tad, doggedly follows the winding pavement. With the engine screaming, the music blasting, the windows down, and my coffee steaming the early morning air, I carefully nursed a little bit of a power slide out of the old truck as we went through one of the tighter curves that topped a hill on the old highway. Just over the peak of the hill and in the tightest part of the curve and out of nowhere, a deer leaped onto the road and began a desperate dash for life down the center of my lane. It was a doe.

Shocked, I got off of the gas and stomped on the brakes. The rear wheels of the truck locked up right away. The tiny Toyota pickup truck skidded and began fishtailing wildly down the road. I fought to keep the truck on the road and out of the ditch. The gap between the front bumper of the truck and the ass of the deer was rapidly closing. In one last effort to avoid the deer, I got off the brake. Freed from the grip of the brakes, the tires regained their bite on the road. I steered sharply to the left and the truck responded by leaping into the left-hand lane. Fortunately, there was no oncoming traffic. Unfortunately, at that exact moment, the deer had the same idea. There was an impact, a very solid impact.

Instinctively I ducked as the deer flew up and over the cab of the truck. I skidded sideways to a stop, blocking the highway. Since we were just around the bend of a sharp curve, I moved the truck to the shoulder of the road so no one would come around the curve and hit it. I got out of the truck and walked back to the deer. It was a doe and she wasn't dead yet. I retrieved my pistol from the truck and put the poor creature out of her misery. I returned to the truck and using the CB radio, I called for the state police. I was going to need an accident report when I filed the insurance claim.

It was broad daylight by the time the state trooper arrived. He parked behind my truck. After giving him my license, registration and all that stuff, we walked over to the deer.

Right away he said, "Wait a minute." Pointing to the bullet hole, he said, "This deer has a gunshot wound."

"She wasn't dead yet. I finished her off with my pistol," I replied.

"You packin'?" the trooper inquired, as his hand neared his weapon.

"No, sir. It's in the truck. I have a rifle in there, too. I live on a ranch. I carry them to deal with feral dogs and coyotes."

The trooper relaxed a little. He knew ranchers did that. He looked at my driver's license for a second. Then he looked at me up and down real good and said, "You Doc's boy? The one who wrecked that golf cart?" I guess I'm never going to live that down.

"No, sir. That was my brother," I lied as the trooper got the little thing out that they use to measure the length of skid marks out of his trunk. At this point, I knew Dad would know about this before I even made it to the farm.

"Doc's not gonna like this," he commented to no one in particular, as he began filling out the accident report.

Looking at me as if he were the grand inquisitor, the trooper asked, "How fast were you going, boy?"

"I was going fifty-five miles an hour, sir," I lied again as he began measuring the length of the skid.

About halfway up the skid mark he stopped, looked at me and said, "Fifty-five miles an hour, huh?"

"Yes, sir. Fifty-five," I replied and we began walking back to the trooper's car.

He finished filling out the report and gave me a copy. Then he asked what I was going to do with the deer. I said I was going to have a BBQ on Saturday at the farm. He asked if Dad would be there, and I told him that he probably would, knowing that there was zero chance that Dad would actually show up. I wasn't dead sure I would be able to actually do the barbecue because I knew Dad was not going to be happy about the truck and I wasn't real keen on driving my Caddy on the gravel roads to get back out to the farm.

Just when you thought it couldn't get worse, karma kicks in and twists the knife. Dad's solution to the truck problem was simple. While the truck was being repaired, I was to live at the farm. Dad has never been one to smile a lot, but I am very sure he smiled as he drove home after depositing me at the farm. On his way back into town, he stopped by Dawson's Store and made an arrangement so I could buy some groceries at the little store a couple of miles from the farm. All this went down so fast, I didn't get a chance to tell

JD, Dezi, or anyone. As far as anyone knew, I had been sucked off the face of the earth by Martians.

If you want to know what lonely is, try watching your ride drive off over the hill leaving you alone on a cattle ranch three miles from the nearest paved road with only a tractor and a horse for transportation. My only means of communication with the outside world was an old CB radio in the trailer. As I watched the dust cloud drift from Dad's car fade away, the only sound was the wind moving in the trees and the occasional moo from the cows in the pasture. I wondered if this might be a good time to try to find religion. They say solitude is good for that.

I went in the trailer and fired up the old CB radio. I needed to get someone to relay a message to JD about the barbecue on Saturday. It took a little while, but I got a hold of someone called "Black Magic," who in turn got a hold of someone called "Spring Fever," who called JD on the phone and delivered the message. I invited Black Magic and Spring Fever to the barbecue. It seemed like the polite thing to do.

Eventually, Saturday arrived. JD got to the farm early. JD got a good laugh out of my predicament. He said, "You said you wanted to be a cowboy. Now's your chance." And then he laughed. I saw very little humor in it. When I looked out over the pastures, all I saw was a lot of work. There were fences to maintain, cattle to tend to and protect. When they are sick, you have to medicate them. You have to manage the fly problem. If you got cows, you got a fly problem. Tending a herd is a hell of a lot of work, and already I was beginning to think twice about my decision to be a cowboy.

JD and I built a fire and got the deer on. He brought a couple of cases of beer with him and a ton of ice. I had ridden Thumbtack, he's my horse, over to Dawson's Grocery and bought a bunch of Wicker's barbecue sauce. It's the only store-bought barbecue sauce worth using. By eight-thirty in the morning, JD and I were kicked back drinking a beer and watching the deer cook. Life was good.

While we tended the fire, we got to talking some. I told him about all the repercussions from the golf tournament. He said he always thought that golf was a bad idea, and he wasn't surprised at all that Dad had marooned me out in the middle of nowhere.

"After all," he said, "everything you touch seems to explode."

I thought for a second. "Well, that's fair," I replied.

I went on to tell JD that, if it weren't for all the work, I really wouldn't mind being out at the farm for the summer, but I dearly wanted to see Dezi again. "She won't take my calls," I said sadly.

97

JD said, "Can you blame her? Y'all were mud rasslin' in front of the whole town." Then he said with a shit-eating grin, "You know, some guys would pay good money to get to do that."

"We weren't rassling, damn it," I said with no small indignation. "I was trying to get her out of the damn mud. I was helping her." Reflecting for just a moment, "I just wish I could talk to her," I added.

JD tossed some grass clippings in the air and said, "Yeah, I think that ship has sunk."

I was thinking that he mangled that expression, but before I could say anything, a dusty, rusty, old pickup truck pulled into the yard. A huge guy got out, and casually walked over to us toting a bottle of some sort.

"How you boys doing? I'm Omar, live over the hill. I heard on the radio that you're having a party," the guy said. He took a big slug off of the bottle, then he presented it to me. "It's kind of a welcome to the neighborhood thing," he said smiling from ear-to-ear. I took a big gulp off of the bottle. I recognized the taste of homemade whisky. "Maybe this cowboy thing isn't so bad after all," I thought.

Well, turns out when I invited Black Magic and Spring Fever to the barbecue over the radio, I was overheard by about thirty other people, too. Over the course of the next couple of hours, one-by-one, new and interesting people arrived at the farm. Each truck brought a cooler of beer, food of some sort, firearms, and two or three new friends. The party took on a whole new aspect.

One of my new friends' name was Enid. In addition to being a working cowboy, he was in a band. He lived down the road about four miles in a trailer under a tree. While his band set up to play, Enid and I talked some. He wanted to know how I came to live out here by myself, being so young and all. I told him the whole damn story starting with the golf cart and ending with the golf tournament. He thought that was pretty funny till he saw that I didn't. He apologized. I told him it was okay. I had figured out that I was gonna be a cowboy. Now I just had to get over Dezi and get used to being lonesome.

Enid commented that girls like doctors a lot more than they like cowboys. If I really wanted her back, he said, I needed to plan on being a doctor. He said that as long as I didn't have a record, it's not really that hard. You just go to school for a long, long time. He stopped and looked at me for a second. "You've never been arrested, have you?" he asked.

"Funny you should ask," I said and laughed. "The first time I got arrested was when I was about eight years old. Me and Walt tried to save Mr. Quarrels from his massive coronary out on the golf course. They put us in jail for a little while, but I don't know what they charged us with. Dad got kicked out of the Country Club. The last time was last year when Sheriff Floyd arrested me for my science fair project. That time it was *Illegal Manufacture of Intoxicating Spirits in a Dry County*."

Enid was shocked. He looked at me intently. He took his hat off and wiped his brow. He shook his head. "Of course, you have a record," he said in disbelief.

"Oh yeah, and that doesn't even include when I got busted stealing the population sign at Black Oak last year." I said with another laugh. "Walt and I got caught by the constable. We had to pay a $25 fine, but we got to keep the sign. It's in Walt's basement now."

"Son, you're screwed. You can't be a doctor. No medical school will take someone with your record. Shit, you can't even be a dentist," Enid said soberly.

"It's not like I'm a convict," I said, in my own defense.

"Yes it is. That is exactly that. You got con-vict-ed of all that stuff. Con-vict or Con-vict-ed. Get it? You are a convict. You probably can't even get in college," he said, the deepest resignation in his voice. "Son, you're screwed." He took a long drink of his beer.

Well, damn. "Dad's not going to like that," I thought. He always said I would be a convict. Now I already had become one, and I never would have known it if Enid hadn't told me. I decided right then and there that if Dad didn't ask, I wasn't gonna tell him. He'll just gloat. There are some things Dad just didn't need to know. It didn't really matter to me. I had already decided to be a cowboy, so not being eligible for medical school didn't bother me that much. Something that did matter to me was Dezi. This hit me right between the eyes. Dezi probably wouldn't ever go out with a convict. The realization that I had probably lost Dezi forever hung around my neck like a millstone. Of course, she would never go out with a convict. Maybe she didn't need to know about that either.

"Cheer up, kid," Enid said. "You can always be a cowboy. You just can't compete on the rodeo circuit. You can work the ranches. They'll take anyone, but the rodeo circuit, you know, they don't allow convicts, except as clowns. You actually could be a rodeo clown."

With that final happy comment, Enid left me on the fence and walked over to the band. In just a few minutes, they started playing. He left me with my thoughts. This really, really sucked. I sat on the fence and listened to the band. All my new friends and neighbors were having a hell of a good time. It was one of the best parties I have ever seen, but now I was pretty bummed out. All I could think about was that I was only sixteen years old and my best career prospect was to be a rodeo clown. I really missed Dezi. Well, the party continued until about two or three in the morning when the beer ran out.

The day after the party was the beginning to a long hot summer. Seems that there is a hell of a lot more to taking care of cattle than what they show you on *Rawhide*. For starters, you have to ride the fences every day and count your cows. If any of the fences are slack or down, you have to fix them. Working barbed wire fences can be a real pain. You have to make sure you are up-to-date on your tetanus shot because you get cut, poked, and scratched up, every day working with barbed wire.

Next, you tend to the herd. You need to get a good look at each cow to make sure none of them are sick. You have to make sure your mineral blocks are good, and your fly dope is good. And you have to prevent the cows from getting pink eye. The best way to prevent getting pink eye loose in the herd is to not let it get started in the first place. That means having good fly control, which means keeping the burlap sacks soaked in diesel oil hanging on the wire in good shape.

Once all that's done, you sometimes have to make hay. There are few jobs on this earth that are more miserable than hauling hay. You always make hay in the hottest part of the summer. At some point, you wind up walking across the pasture picking up bales of hay and tossing them on a wagon or a pickup truck. Usually, one guy drives the truck real slow and the other guys throw the hay on the truck and stack it. I didn't have any help, so I drove the truck to a spot, then I got out and loaded every near-by bale. I'd move the truck and do it again. You do that about a million times and those bales get pretty damn heavy. After that, you have to stack they hay in a hay barn. And this is an absolute truth. The tin roof in a hay barn is hotter than anything except the surface of the sun. If you touch your bare back to it while stacking hay, you won't do it twice.

On a farm or ranch, you are never done. There is always more to do. Sometimes, you just need to take a break from everything and go visit someone. I used to ride Thumbtack, my horse, over to Omar's house for a beer every now and then. It wasn't real far. I went to Enid's trailer once, only once.

Enid, in addition to being a working cowboy and having a band, was a semi-pro bull rider. It was good that he had another part-time gig because, honestly, his band sucks. At his place he had a bull riding arena all set up. That one time I went to see Enid was a learning experience for me. Just like there's more to taking care of cattle than *Rawhide* would lead you to believe, there's more to bull riding than watching it on TV will show you, too.

On this particular day, Enid and his best friend, Roscoe, were drinking beer and having fun riding his bull. For a working cowboy, I noticed that Enid seemed to have an awful lot of time on his hands. I was never caught up over at my place, and he never seemed to work at his. The bull was the only animal I ever saw there, other than three broken-down horses and some chickens. I had my doubts about just how much of a cowboy Enid was. I think he may have been a rodeo bum.

Regardless, I had a pretty good time helping with the whole bull riding thing. Seems that there's a lot of prep work to get ready to ride a bull. When someone is actually riding the bull, there are a number of things that have to be taken care of. One, you need someone to open the gate on the chute to let the bull out. That's a pretty easy job. There's a rope you just pull and the gate swings to you. You never even have to get off the fence. You also need someone to act as the clown. The clown job is to distract the bull so the rider, having been thrown off the bull, has a chance to get up and escape over the fence without the bull running him down. The clown job is probably the most important in the whole thing. When a cowboy comes off the bull, it's the clown who keeps him safe until he escapes. Being the clown is a very important role.

It was a hot day, so in the interest of staying hydrated, we were doing some serious beer drinking. At first, I helped get the bull in the chute. You have to learn these things one at a time. Next, I learned to operate the gate. That was pretty cool. In between Enid and Roscoe taking turns riding, I'd down a beer or two and do what I needed to do to help out. I noticed that each time I opened the gate, the bull did pretty much the same thing. He'd make a huge leap sideways out of the chute. He'd get his head down and bow up his back and start jumping up and kicking out with his back legs. Then he would start to spin clockwise, or sometimes counterclockwise, while jumping up and down and kicking at the same time. You only had to stay on for eight seconds. After time was up, you could hop off and make a dash for the fence while the clown distracted the bull. Enid and Roscoe took turns being the rider and the clown.

I was setting on the fence when a little voice in the back of my head whispered, "You can do this."

I have heard this little voice before. This little voice was not a friend of mine. Listening to that little bastard usually leads to pain, suffering, and bleeding.

A few minutes later, the little bastard whispered again. "You know exactly what he's going to do."

I had to admit to myself that this was true. I thought as I drank another beer. I did know exactly what the bull was going to do. He did the same thing every time. Enid and Roscoe knew this. That's why they were so good at staying on him. Knowing this, I figured that it shouldn't be very difficult to anticipate the moves and to stay balanced. I was pretty damn good on a pony. I should be able to do this.

"I might could do this," I said to myself as I finished a beer.

"You got this," the little bastard confidently whispered in my ear.

"I got this," I said out loud, as I crushed the empty beer can and tossed it in the pile with the other empty beer cans.

Enid and Roscoe were all in on me riding Satan. That was the bull's name, Satan. In no time, Satan is back in the chute and the riding rig is ready. I pulled my hat down nearly to my ears so that maybe it wouldn't come off. With my right hand in the handle, we wrap the remaining part of the rig around my hand several times. I snug up on my hand and lean forward, and a little to the right, anticipating that first jump.

When I had worked the gate, the rider would look at me. Then the rider would very deliberately nod at me to let me know he was ready for me to open the gate. Sitting on the bull, I was growing less confident by the second. I looked up at Enid for some encouragement. Unfortunately, Enid apparently had his own way of doing things. Simply looking at Enid was apparently the sign for Enid to open the gate to the chute. There was no nod involved.

You can imagine my surprise.

Sitting on a bull is unlike anything else you may have done in your entire life unless, of course, you have straddled a rocket. This two-thousand-pound monster is not in a good mood. He does not like his lot in life. When you are sitting on him, it feels like you are sitting on a living, breathing mountain. The animal's muscles are like coiled steel. Each twitch, each breath, each snort can be felt in your bones. It resonates through you. Your very innards are trembling.

It dawned on me that this may not have been a good idea.

When Enid opened the gate, the Satan exploded. He didn't actually explode, but he leaped out of the chute with the velocity of a rocket shot. I hung on for dear life with my right arm. The bull landed that first leap, and he really stuck the landing. I would give him a ten for that landing. I was expecting him to begin his stationary jumping with his head down. I saw him duck his head down, but then he did something odd. Instead of jumping up and down like he was supposed to, he began to leap forward and kick his feet out behind him. My right hand was securely in the handle of the bull riding rig. With each leap, I was amazed to find that I could feel my arm bones moving in my shoulder socket. Using my bad shoulder was probably not the smartest thing. Finally, he stopped the forward leaps. I expected and was prepared for a spin clockwise. Imagine my surprise when it was a counterclockwise spin that he started. I was starting to come unseated now, and the bull knew it. They can tell these things. With a grand finale leap forward and a monster kick, I came flying off the back of the beast like a bead of sweat. When Enid and Roscoe departed the bull, they did so gracefully and usually landed under control. I was launched off of that monster like snot slung out of his nose. I landed awkwardly on the hard dirt. I was pretty sure I busted a couple of ribs.

Roscoe was supposed to be the clown, but he and Enid were laughing too hard to do much of anything. Let me just say, here and now, that Roscoe is fired. I made it over the fence by the grace of God with an assist from Satan. I thought I had a pretty good ride. You're supposed to stay on eight seconds, but according to Enid, I almost got to one.

I pondered the bull ride, while I was out riding the fences and checking the pasture a few days later. I decided that I was done with Satan. I was a little banged up, but I think I learned my lesson. I'll never ride a bull again. In addition to that, I learned that there are lunatics in this world who will encourage you to do stupid things. Not all of these lunatics live in your head. Some of the lunatics live in a trailer under a tree on Crowley's Ridge.

On my ride, it became clear that the front pastures were looking rough from the drought. After riding through them for a bit, I decided that I was going to have to move our cattle to another pasture, the back pasture. I didn't want them to burn up the pasture they were in. We really, really needed rain.

Before I moved them to a different pasture, I always rode the fences to make sure that all the fences were up. On this ride, I found that there was a section that was down, so I set about fixing it. It took a while. I was hot and sweaty when I finished the repair. It was right at lunch time. A little of a breeze kicked up, and in the distance, I could see that there were clouds building. I sniffed the breeze for rain, but all I could smell was hamburgers. Someone pretty close was cooking hamburgers. I figured I could follow my nose to find out who was cooking hamburgers. It shouldn't be hard to talk them out of a cool drink of water and maybe a burger. At my party, I had met everyone in a five-mile radius. I figured it was a sure thing that I had already met whoever was cooking burgers. So, Thumbtack and I went out the rear gate, and followed the smell of hamburgers.

We followed our noses. It wasn't too far down the dirt road, maybe three-quarters of a mile. At that point, the road veered off to the left, but the smell came from down a path straight in front of us. It was a fairly small path that would be a tight fit for a pickup truck. If you didn't know this place was there, you'd never find it. We came up on what appeared to be a very dilapidated, old country store set back in the deep shade of the trees. It had room for maybe three pickups to park, if they could get down the path from the road to the store. Looking at it, I thought that if the termites quit holding hands, the place would fall down. A rusty sign with three bullet holes in it, told me I was at Ray's Last Chance. The smell of hamburgers lured me toward the door.

I tied Thumbtack in the shade and made sure he had plenty of water. It was deep shade, so he would be comfortable and cool while I went inside.

I paused before entering. I brushed some of the dust off of me, took my hat off and wiped my face with my bandanna. I opened the door and stepped in. The cold air inside the place hit me so hard it made me dizzy, lightheaded. Air conditioning is a good thing, a very good thing. It was dark inside, and it took a second for my eyes to adjust.

"Come in, have a seat at the bar," a voice called from somewhere in the dark barroom. I walked across the old wood floor to the bar. It creaked a little as I crossed the room. The windows were blacked out and had bars, I noted. I have always made a note of escape routes for some reason, and those bars on the windows made me think this might be something of a fire trap. An old woman emerged from the darkness. Before I could ask a coke, she set a beer in a frosty mug on the bar in front of me. I hadn't even seen her draw the beer.

"What do you want on your burger?" she asked as she turned back toward the kitchen.

Without waiting for my answer, she glanced back and winked at me. Looking toward the kitchen door she shouted, "Cheese, mustard, onion, and pickle."

"You're Doc's boy, aren't you?" the old woman asked. "Sorry I missed the party," she added in a way that told me she wasn't really sorry she'd missed the party at all. She walked over to the old juke box and dropped a couple of coins in. She played an old Hank Williams' song.

Leaning back against the juke box, she said, "I was wondering how long it would be before you'd show up."

I took a long drink from my beer, as I wondered if she was going to do both sides of the conversation the whole time, or if I would get to contribute at some point. It was one of the coldest beers I had ever had. On this hot day, it went down well. I looked at the old woman. She looked older than Moses but moved like a much younger person. She must have been quite a looker in her day. A grunt from the kitchen signaled that my burger was ready. She disappeared into the kitchen to retrieve it.

I took the opportunity to look around a little. In the darkness of the room, the whole place looked like a scene from a black-and-white movie. Everything in this place looked like it was a hundred years old. I wondered how, with all the dust, this place ever passed a health department inspection, not that that would stop me from eating the hamburger. I could see faded certificates of some sort on the wall over by the old jukebox. I looked at it for just a minute. My grandfather had one just like it in his bar. This one sounded a lot better than his did. Hank was singing one of his church songs, "I Saw the Light," I think. Who in the hell plays church music in a bar?

The old woman was back with my burger and another beer.

"So, I hear you are Doc's little pain in the ass," she said as she slid the plate to me. The burger looked great, but the fries appeared to be somewhat questionable.

"So, that's how this is going to go?" I thought to myself.

"Relax, I have known you your entire life," she said as if she heard my thoughts.

I really didn't know what to say to that. Finally, I looked at her. I figured she must have been one of Dad's patients down in Mississippi. I swallowed the first bite of what is probably the best hamburger I have ever had.

Finally, to answer her question, I said, "Yes, ma'am. I guess I am. I'm 'Doc's little pain in the ass.'"

We had a good conversation. Just like with Enid, she had to hear the whole story beginning with the golf cart, and then all the way through to hitting the deer. She laughed real hard a couple of times and slapped her knee. Every now and then, she stopped me and asked a question or two.

"Shit just sort of happens to you, doesn't it," she said as she lit a cigarette. She looked at me for confirmation. Looking away and blowing smoke rings in the air, she casually said, "I believe someone has put a curse on you, Billy Boy."

"A what?" I asked, shocked more about what she had called me than about the curse thing.

"A curse, Billy Boy. Bad juju. Someone has laid an Evil on you," she expounded.

"You mean I wasn't born unlucky?" I countered, as I wondered why in the hell she was calling me that.

"Not a chance," she very confidently replied. Her voice and her body language was full of assurance. She said this as if she knew for certain.

"Well, that would explain a lot," I said through a mouth full of cheeseburger. "You know, I burnt the house down once," I added.

"That was different," she said as she smiled and her eyes twinkled. "That wasn't from the curse. That was because a little boy had a big sneeze."

"Who have you pissed off, Billy Boy?" she said as she leaned down to me on the bar. Her calling me that name had caught me by surprise. I hadn't told her my name and no one calls me "Billy Boy." The only person, who had ever called me Billy Boy, was that big bastard at his trial when he said he was gonna gut me and make me watch while he fed my liver to the fish. He only called me Billy Boy because he didn't know my real name. Her green eyes looked deeply into my eyes. It was like she could see my thoughts in my head. "Who have you pissed off, Billy Boy?" she repeated.

I thought for a second.

Her eyes were soft when she asked that question again. She had gray hair that went everywhere. Her skin was absolutely white with few wrinkles, and if I were guessing, I'd say she had never had a suntan in her life. Even being old as the hills, her skin looked young and soft. "Billy Boy," she said, "Who is out to get you?"

"That," I thought to myself, "could be a really long list."

All of a sudden, it hit me like lightning. I knew why I had bad luck. It had to be the big bastard. That big bastard must have had someone put a curse on me! I must have lit up because the old woman reacted and said, "Who, Billy Boy? Who is it?"

I told the old lady the whole story about being kidnapped out of the Desoto jail by a bank robber years ago. She listened intently when I told her about crashing the sheriff's car, about Uncle Johnny's funeral, and finally about how Elvis beat up the big bastard before my brother knocked him out with an ax handle. I still shake some when I tell the story, and she noticed it. As I finished, I realized I didn't know who I was talking to.

"Ma'am, excuse me, but I don't know your name," I said.

"Angel Ray, sweet boy. All my friends call me Angel," she said. "This," she paused and gestured around with her arm as if she were presenting the place, "is my Last Chance."

"That man has put a curse on you, Billy Boy. He has no proxy. It was him. He himself put this curse on you," she said sounding very confident and assured. "He's a bad man," she added as she turned toward the beer coolers. She paused and lifted her head up and a little to the side as if listening to something distant. "He lives, you know," she added again, as almost an afterthought as she turned to give me yet another beer.

"You are going to need to lift that curse," she said. "Your life will not get better until you lift that curse."

"He might live right now," I thought, "but not for long. He's all out of appeals and at trial, he got the death penalty for killing the bouncers at the Dixie Chicken Gentleman's Club. If he hasn't already fried in the chair, it wouldn't be long till he did." But there was no way she could know that.

I told Miss Angel that I didn't know how to lift a curse. I didn't have a talisman mouse or nothing.

"A what?" she asked incredulously. I told her about Sweet Pea's stuffed mouse and how it worked. I confessed that I was kind of afraid to go into Voodoo Village to get one.

"That mouse has no luck. Hell, if the damn mouse had any luck it wouldn't be dead, stuffed, and getting carried around in your sister's purse," she said with a wink.

"I knew it," I thought. "That damn mouse is just a damn mouse!"

Resuming with a much more optimistic tone, she said, "Not to worry, young man. You can lift the curse and you don't need a stupid mouse." She took me by the hands and, again, looked deeply into my eyes and said softly, "All you need is faith."

"Faith? That's all? Faith in what?" I asked.

"That, my young friend, is what you must figure out," she said. She gave my hands a good squeeze and she turned away. Walking into the kitchen she said, "Once you have faith, the curse will be lifted. Now, finish your burger and go home. A storm is coming and it's a long ride. You've got your gun?"

"Yes, ma'am," I said wondering how she knew I carried a gun.

"Good. Finish and go."

"But I haven't paid my tab," I protested.

"Pay me next time you see me, Billy Boy. Now go! Time is short!" She turned and retreated into the darkness.

In the distance, I heard a rumble of thunder.

Deliverance

And a hell of a storm it was! I barely got back to my trailer before it really got going. The lightning started while I was halfway across our middle pasture. If you want to really live on the edge, just try riding a horse across a bald pasture in a thunderstorm. That will put the fear of God in you. The thunder rolled across the pastures like waves breaking on a rugged coastline. It was that deep, hard, innard shaking thunder. The wind started to come up while I crossed that last pasture. I had to hold my hat on.

Powerful gusts were really putting the trees in the tree line to the test. The old barn rattled in the wind as I was tended to Thumbtack in the barn. Raindrops the size of tennis balls began falling and made a hell of a racket on the barn roof, but the hail didn't start until I was in the trailer. A hailstorm in a trailer is something everyone should experience exactly one time. It made me understand what being inside a snare drum would be like. Like riding a bull, if you have any brains at all, one experience of being in a trailer in a bad storm is enough. The lightning seemed to hit mere feet from the trailer every fifteen seconds. Gale force winds beat the sides trailer unmercifully. Despite being securely anchored to the ground, I could feel my trailer rock in the wind some. That flash-bang lightning that you get when the storm sits right on top of you really gets your attention. They say that lightning never strikes the same place twice. I figure that's because that place it struck ain't there anymore.

It stormed all night. I knew that for sure because I stayed up all night. No one in Northeast Arkansas who lives in a trailer will go to sleep during a storm. Trailers are, after all, just tornado bait. In the morning, just as the rain was stopping, the sun was coming up. Off in the distance there was just a hint of a rainbow. Being mostly color blind, I can only see part of a rainbow, but sure enough. There was a rainbow after the storm.

The drought was broken and the pastures came back to life and I didn't have to move the herd into the far pasture. With no cattle there, I didn't have cause to be over by Ray's the rest of the summer. I thought about what Angel had said a lot. That was one weird old lady. All I need, she'd said, was faith. That may be true, but I also owe her $5.50 for the burger and three beers.

Being a rancher is hard work. It is a lot harder work than I was interested in doing. Rain or shine, the herd has to come first. After the herd, you take care of your horse. Your needs come last, if they come at all. By the end of the summer, I had learned a lot. I knew that I didn't want to be a cowboy. I understood that there were a lot of things in this world that are more important than self. I really appreciated a good meal. I still didn't like algebra, but I was looking forward to moving back home, starting school again. I missed Dezi madly, but I had accepted that she was lost to me. That's the price you pay for being a convict.

When the truck was finally repaired, I had some mobility. That was a welcomed improvement. With the truck I had the ability to make a run to Red Onion to get beer. Red Onion was a little place on the state line with Missouri where they were less than diligent about checking IDs for the purchase of beer. This was a good thing because while the truck was being repaired, I was dependent on others to make my beer runs for me. Now that I was mobile, the very first thing I did was to drive over to pay my tab at Ray's Last Chance. Try as I might, I could never find the place. I drove all the little dirt roads around the far pasture, but I couldn't find the place.

Right before school started, Dad came out and we had a visit. He wanted me to keep living at the farm. Mom, it seems, was doing much better and he thought it would be best if I stayed at the farm. I think the truck had been repaired for quite a while but that Dad had thought it best to leave me marooned at the farm. With school starting, he had to either have me move back to the house or give up the truck.

As the fates would have it, Dezi and I were in the same geometry class. On that first day, we were assigned seats and just like last year, we were seated almost beside each other. I couldn't look at her. She wouldn't look at me. This sucked. This really, really sucked. This went on all week. Not a word was spoken. Not a glance.

As was the tradition at Jonbur High, there was a school mixer scheduled for that first Friday of school. We were still going to school at the fairgrounds on account of the tornado that blew the high school away a year and a half ago. The mixer was held in one of the exhibition buildings at the fairgrounds. The band was set up in the building. If you ever get the opportunity to listen to a loud rock band playing in an empty metal building, just skip it. You'll thank me later.

I have never been one for loud music, so JD and I hung around outside near the front gate with some other guys. I had parked my truck close to the gate. While we were shooting the breeze out there, we were secretly drinking beer out of our Minuteman Hamburgers cups. We talked about dove season and girls. It would open soon, and most of the guys already had their spots picked out for opening day. JD was madly in love with a pretty blond named Summer. Moody wanted to know if JD had seen Summer's tan lines yet. We all thought that was pretty funny. Well, everyone except JD.

While we were talking, a police car came roaring up. It skidded to a halt right by the entrance to the fairgrounds. A cop jumped out and dashed into the exhibition hall where the dance was. JD, finishing a big drink from his Minuteman cup, casually observed, "Someone must have started a fight."

Pearson disagreed. "For a fight, they always send three or four cars." Bradley nodded in agreement. Pearson and Bradley were our resident experts on building engines and cops. They both had plenty of experience dealing with both, so I figured they ought to know.

Moments later, the cop emerged from the exhibition hall with one of the guys from my neighborhood in tow. Harold was being arrested for being drunk, but it didn't look like he was very drunk. He was handcuffed and walking okay. JD noted that Harold's mouth seemed to be working fine, too. JD hollered over and told him to shut up. If the cop hadn't announced he was being arrested for being drunk, no one would have figured out what he was getting busted for. He just didn't look or act drunk. "Maybe he was stoned," I suggested to the guys.

Harold was a good guy, and no one wanted him to go to jail. JD and I went to work trying to get the cop to let us take Harold home, but the cop would not have any of it. While we were talking to the cop, Misty ran up and laid a massive, passionate kiss on Harold. Misty was a very pretty girl, much out of Harold's league, but one of his friends nonetheless. I thought that running up and giving him a kiss like he was going off to war was a bit odd even for Misty. Well, it turns out she had an ulterior motive. She did that so she could slip a penny into Harold's mouth from her mouth. As you probably know, if you have penny under your tongue when you blow on the breathalyzer, it won't register any alcohol. Unfortunately, Harold didn't know what the hell was happening. Misty just grabbed him and laid a big one on him, he didn't even see her coming. When she slipped the penny into his mouth, he almost swallowed it. He gagged and choked on it. He then proceeded to throw up on the cop.

It was apparent right then that Harold indeed had been drinking, probably Boone's Farm Strawberry Hill. The cop was not amused at all, and immediately shoved Harold into the backseat of his car. He slammed the door shut. JD and I kept talking to the cop, trying to get him to give Harold to us. It was a lost cause, a done deal. Harold was going to jail. The cop ended our conversation and got in the car. He put it in gear and drove about ten feet and then stopped. He jumped out of the car. He jerked open the back door and looked in the backseat. Harold was gone! He was not in the back seat of the police car. All hell broke loose. The cop got on his radio and in just a minute or two about twenty cops descended on the fairgrounds with sirens going and lights flashing to search for Harold.

JD and I were standing there beside my truck, not under arrest, but definitely detained for questioning when Dezi drove by. Our pucker factor was significantly enhanced by the presence of our Minuteman cups at our feet which were still full of very illegal beer. Using my foot, I nudged both of our Minuteman cups somewhat out of sight under the truck. Dezi looked at me and JD as she drove slowly by. She smiled at me and winked. Well, I thought, that's an improvement. She might just be rubbing my predicament it in a little, but she looked at me and a wink is communication. I'll take that any day. JD and I had to talk to about a dozen cops and one detective. They said they could arrest us for helping a fugitive from justice to escape. I pointed out that we were standing there with the arresting cop the whole time. We couldn't have done anything at all. The cops demanded to know what the fugitive's name was. We told them we didn't know. They were dead set on getting a full name out of us, but we played dumb. Finally, they let us go, but they said they would "keep an eye on us."

One of the cops eyed JD real hard. He looked JD straight in the eye, testing to see when JD would look away. JD stayed the course and neither looked away nor blinked. Just before he looked away, the cop said, "Boy, I foresee a really uncomfortable future for you at the Penal Farm."

JD didn't understand what he meant. I watched JD as he thought it over. I saw the light bulb flash over his head. He hands instinctively covered "the family jewels." JD went pale as a sheet as he reached a terrible conclusion about what a Penal Farm was. I figured out right quick what he was thinking. The first time I heard the term "Penal Farm," I had the same thought. I shook JD and said to him, "Relax! It's okay! The Penal Farm ain't what you think it is."

At school on Monday, Harold came by to say thanks. I said that I didn't know what he was thanking us for because we didn't get him out. After he threw up on the cop, the cop was really pissed and shoved him in the back seat of the police car. Despite our best efforts, at that point he was going to jail.

"Yeah," he said. "That was pretty funny. Dezi had the door on the other side of the cop car open. I went in one door and out the other," he said with a big grin. "She shut her door at the same time the cop slammed his door," he said with a laugh. "The cop never even got my name."

"No shit!" JD said in utter amazement. "They kept trying to get us to give you up."

"Dezi said she gave you 'the wink' on the way out to let you know all was okay," he continued.

"Son of a bitch," I said. "I thought she was just winking at me for fun because the cops were hassling us." JD and I both were still factoring this in, and in something of a state of shock over this when I saw Dezi walking up staring straight at me. She didn't even blink. She walked right up to me.

"So, will you talk to me now? Am I forgiven?" she demanded with her hands on her hips and her head defiantly high.

"Will I talk to you? Forgiven? Forgiven for what?" I exclaimed. "I've been trying to get a hold of you for three months! You won't answer the phone," I said.

"Really? You called? Liar! I was home every night. You didn't call not once!" Dezi said as she burned through me with eyes bluer than the fall sky.

"I was stuck at the farm all summer without a phone or a car," I pleaded. "I called from the pay phone at Dawson's store every time I went there for groceries or lunch. It had the only phone I could get to. No one ever answered. Hell, I used the same dime the whole summer." Until then, I had never thought about that. I always put the dime on top of the phone so I wouldn't lose it. Unless someone borrowed it, it's still there.

Dezi gave a long exhale. Her look softened. She smiled a little. "No one was at home during the day because everyone was working, silly rabbit," she said. "Mom and Dad were at the shop and I had a summer job at the Fitness Center. I thought you were ignoring me."

Then, looking at me quizzically, she asked, "Why were you stuck at the farm?"

I told Dezi the story about how Dad thought it might be easier on Mom if I worked at the farm and then, of course, I told her about wrecking the truck on the first week. It really seems like my life is just one long story of disaster after disaster. When we figured out that we just couldn't connect all summer because of our circumstances, we both had a good laugh. I think she was a relieved as I was. I had thought she was angry with me about the mud at the Country Club, and she had thought the same of me. I told her how much I missed her and she smiled that smile that makes me stupid. I felt like a new man. Life was good. Dezi and I hugged for the first time since I pulled her out of the mud. It felt so good. It seems to be true that absence does make the heart grow fonder.

One thing hung on me like a wet blanket. I was a convict. I decided I would wait for the right time to tell Dezi about that. I really didn't have to tell her that just now, not at this moment.

Harold and JD just stood there listening while all this was going on. Finally, JD had enough and said, "You two, get a room!"

Dezi blushed a little.

Harold took this as an opportunity to jump in and invite JD, Dezi, and me, to a meeting of a group he was in. I was afraid it was going to be some lame self-help group or a group for kids with troubles, but he claimed that it wasn't like that at all. It was a search and rescue unit of some sort. It didn't have a name yet. Harold called it The Unit, and said that it's fun.

JD didn't have anything better to do and Dezi wanted to go to the meeting. I was going to go anywhere Dezi was going to go. JD, Harold, Dezi, and I, all went to the meeting that night. Lo and behold, Harold had been telling the truth. It was a lot of fun. This really was a Marine Search and Rescue unit. It was set up by a former Marine gunnery sargent named

Carl Grimmit. He didn't look like a Marine. He looked like a nice guy.

These guys did a lot of the stuff you used to see Sunday afternoons on *The Wide World of Sports*. This outfit did all kinds of stuff. Ever see Jacques Cousteau? Want to scuba dive? This outfit scuba dived. Ever watch them climb the Matterhorn on TV? These guys learned how to climb up cliffs and rappel back down with a guy on a stretcher. They also learned how to search for plane crashes and lost hunters. They learned how to search for drowning victims and how to recover evidence from ponds and lakes for police. Want to be an EMT? These guys had an EMT training program. They went camping just to go camping. This was the best thing ever.

On this particular night, the group was to take a vote to pick the name it wanted to be known by. There were two choices. Carl's Commandos or Grimmit's Guerrillas. We all joined that night and got to participate in the vote to name the group. We officially became Grimmit's Guerrillas, Marine Search and Rescue, but everyone just called it The Unit.

Over the next few months, we did a lot of fun things. Mr. Grimmet was big on training. If you weren't a certified diver, you became a certified diver. Everyone became a Red Cross lifeguard. If you didn't know anything about body work or engines, no sweat. You were about to learn. We all took the class and became Sky Warn Storm Spotters. A lot of kids were in a class and became certified Emergency Medical Techs.

When we joined, JD and I were already certified divers, but we weren't certified lifeguards. We had to take a class right away. It was late fall when the class began. It just so happened that we were in the same Red Cross lifesaving class as some of the girls from school. At first, we that this was too good to be true. We knew there would be a lot of wrestling with girls in the class because one of the main drills was dragging each other out of the pool. JD and I were both very excited about the prospect of wrestling in the water with some very curvy girls who were wearing skintight tank suits. That was all we could think of. JD and I went into this thinking was it the best of all worlds.

In each exercise, one person is designated as the victim, and another person is the rescuer. The victim is in the water pretending to be a panicked swimmer. The rescuer swims out and rescues the victim using whatever technique we just learned. The victim is supposed to struggle against the rescuer as a panicked swimmer would. The rescuer has to get control of the victim and get them out of danger and out of the water.

At first, the instructor had JD and me working together. I would be the victim once, then we would switch and JD would be the victim. This was not what we had envisioned. Against each other, we merely went through the motions. We put up half-hearted efforts at being the panicked swimmer. It wasn't very hard for either of us to rescue the other. We were, after all, just going through the motions. This was not the fun we had imagined.

After a couple of classes of that, the instructor was satisfied that everyone had mastered the basic mechanics and concepts of the rescue techniques. At that point, things changed up some. She threw JD and me to the sharks.

As I said, all we could think of was that we were about to get to wrestle nearly-naked girls in a pool. That's all that was in our teenaged minds, "wrestling with nearly naked girls." It never occurred to us that these particular girls were in top-notch physical condition, incredibly flexible, amazingly agile, and just a little insane. They were the gymnastics team.

When we began trying to rescue the girls, I cannot describe the chaos that ensued. They turned into eye gouging, nut kicking, kidney punching, hair pulling maniacs the very second the rescue began. Their style of battle was completely uninhibited. They assaulted you from every angle using arms, legs and every inch of their supremely conditioned and very curvy bodies. It didn't matter whether we were the victim or the rescuer, JD and I were getting mauled multiple times a night during the last four training sessions.

On the first night of real exercises, I watched JD, despite his best efforts to escape, get pulled out very roughly by the hair of his head. I got a haircut the next day. After the four nights of wrestling with the girls, JD and I were fairly beat up and more than a little contrite. We had, after all, just been beat up by a bunch of curvy girls in a swimming pool. We came away from the training with a lot more respect for the gymnasts. We were a lot wiser, too, and not just about water rescue stuff. We agreed that no one need know the details of our experience with this.

Our last hope for gratuitous physical contact of some sort was dashed when the instructor brought out a CPR dummy for us to practice on. To say we were crestfallen is not nearly a strong enough word. We were defeated. We had zero interest in performing CPR on the dummy. We wanted to perform it on as many of the girls as we could. In the end, we learned CPR on the dummy and passed the course.

We also learned repelling much the same way, except this time from Mr. Grimmet. Becky pranced down the face of the cliff like Tinker Bell. When it was my turn to learn, I carefully and patiently explained to him that I had a profound fear of heights. He explained to me that he didn't care. Mr. Grimmet could make things very clear with just a look.

Everyone learned rappelling and climbing. Despite my fear of heights, I learned it. I'm still scared of heights, but I can get down a hundred-foot face of a cliff without a second thought. It's all in the training. Harold got really good at it. We used to laugh and claim that Harold could climb up a plate glass window. In fact, he very nearly could.

Sky Warn training was pretty interesting. We learned all about the processes and responsibilities of storm spotting. The way things work is like this. The county had an old World War II radar unit set up at Storm Center. When storms were coming, they fired up the radar and would watch for "hook echos." A funnel cloud will produce a hook echo on the radar scope. When they had a hook echo, Center would contact storm spotters near that location. They would give the spotters a compass heading. The spotters would look at the countryside on that heading, and report whether or not there was a funnel cloud. If there was a funnel cloud, the spotters would report details such as direction of travel, whether or not it was on the ground, and other similar stuff.

The Unit somehow acquired an old Army 6X truck. A 6X is pronounced "Six-by." I don't know why, it just is. It may be because it is a six-wheel-drive truck. Anyway, a 6X is a troop truck. It sort of looks like a giant pickup with benches down the sides of the back, and a canvas cover. You see them in war movies all the time. We went to work on it. Our 6X had a blown engine, so JD recruited Bradley and Pearson to join the unit. They began tearing the engine down as the rest of us began working on the body of the thing. It was decided that we should paint it in the color scheme of Rommel's Afrika Korps. We spent weeks repairing the dents and bends in the old body of the truck. As we neared the point when we could paint the truck, we had a problem we needed to solve. We didn't have any paint, and we didn't have any money to buy paint with. We were kind of stuck.

JD, Dezi, and I, were having coffee at Shoney's one afternoon just brainstorming about how the post could raise some money. There's just not a lot of things that we could do. About the only thing anyone could think of was directing cars parking at the football games, and the college already had someone helping with that. JD had looked into getting paint. It was going to take about $150 of custom automotive paint to paint the 6X. If it wasn't a custom color, it wouldn't be so expensive. We wanted a special cream color because that was the base color for the Afrika Korps paint scheme. We were just sitting there thinking this over when a Sealtest milk truck stopped on Caraway Road to make a turn. Gazing at the cream-colored Sealtest milk truck, I had a flash of inspiration.

The Sealtest truck was painted in the exact color that we needed! At the next meeting of the Guerrillas, we discussed this some. It was decided that we should approach the Sealtest folks to see if they would consider helping us with the paint. Harold and Bell were assigned to the task. Pearson and Bradley reported that the motor was a disaster. It could not be rebuilt, it was going to take a new engine. Again, having no money to work with was proving to be a problem.

Well, fast forward about a month, our membership continued to grow, and somehow, we've got paint for the truck, and the engine was magically healed. Harold and Bell had come through with the paint, and somehow, without buying any parts other than new spark plugs, the 6X's engine had been magically healed. Harold and Bell didn't talk about how they got Sealtest to cough up the paint, and Pearson and Bradley weren't saying anything about the engine. Dezi smelled a skunk.

It took a little doing, but we found out the truth. Actually, it just took some beer and a campfire. Harold and Bell said they knew that the folks at Sealtest wouldn't willingly donate paint to us. Bell knew Becky, the granddaughter of the guy who ran the shop for Sealtest. Bell said the Becky was pretty cool, but that her grandfather was an ass. She said that it was a sure thing that they would get turned down if they asked for a donation of five gallons of paint. The storeroom at the Sealtest shop was in the very back of the shop. There could be no sneaking in and sneaking out with five gallons of paint. The shop was very well-secured, so burglary was out of the question. Harold said that left only one option.

Becky was pretty cool, and definitely a looker. She wasn't sure at first that she wanted to join The Unit, but Harold and Bell explained all the fun we had to her and convinced her to come to a meeting. The meeting, she said, was filled with lunatics, but that we were her kind of lunatics, so she was all in. Very quickly, she became a member and two weeks later, we had five gallons of cream-colored automotive paint and five gallons of primer. Who knew Becky understood auto painting?

It wasn't too long after that the JD and I heard the rest of the story. Harold and Bell didn't tell us this part. In exchange for the paint and primer, Becky swung a deal with Harold and Bell. They would medicate her cat for her. Becky had a long-haired cat of some sort named Sarah, who had some sort of weird skin mite. It took a special medicine to get rid of the mite, and Becky, try as she might, could not medicate Sarah.

This particular medication was supposed to be dissolved in a water bath. The animal being treated was supposed to be thoroughly bathed in the bath, then thoroughly rinsed with fresh water. Becky had tried to bathe Sarah, but the cat clawed the hell out of her and escaped. Sarah was a large cat and well able to defend herself. Becky wasn't even able to get the cat into the water at all. Becky worked a deal for Harold and Bell to bathe Sarah, in exchange for her acquiring the paint for the 6X.

As anyone might imagine, the idea of bathing this cat did not phase Harold and Bell at all. It was, after all, just a cat. How hard could it be? The plan was they would get some long gloves to protect themselves from the claws, and just submerge the cat in the kitchen sink filled with medicated water. It was thought that this would be a man-handling situation, no finesse involved, just grab the cat and dunk the cat. Not real hard.

Well, they were wrong.

Harold filled the kitchen sink, and Bell caught the cat. As they entered the kitchen, the cat saw the sink. All hell broke loose. Sarah got loose before Bell even got halfway to the sink. Just so he would remember it, she clawed the hell out of Bell before she made a beeline out of the bathroom. Harold was shocked at how quickly this happened. They retreated to rethink this. This was going to be more of a problem than they had anticipated. Creativity was needed.

The problem was a tough one. Even if you managed to submerge the cat and rub her long enough to make sure she was thoroughly soaked with the medicated water, you still had to rinse the cat. The directions said it was absolutely vital to ensure that the cat was well-rinsed. Harold and Bell were stuck for a while on this. They were hanging out at Minuteman Hamburgers thinking it through when Harold had a brainstorm.

They went back to Becky's house and caught the cat. This was easier said than done. Sarah knew what they were up to, so she avoided them. Despite their best efforts, Sarah was able to elude capture for several days. Finally, Bell had an idea.

Bell bought a couple of mice at the pet store. The pet store stocked mice for people who fed them to their snakes. What sick person has a snake for a pet? Anyway, Bell bought two mice. The plan was to tie the mice to an inverted laundry basket propped up with a stick. The idea was that Sarah would not be able to resist two mice out in the open like that. When she went for the mice, the laundry basket would fall and trap her. Sure enough, that is pretty much how we caught her. The mice, unfortunately, got away. Becky never needs to know about that.

Harold, wearing huge and protective gloves, casually walked into the bathroom holding Sarah. He held the cat up so she could see herself in the mirror. He was gentle with the cat as he turned to leave the bathroom. Just as he passed the toilet, he slam dunked the cat into the toilet and Bell tossed in the medicine. Harold closed the lid, trapping the cat in the toilet.

At this point, the cat went absolutely wild in the toilet. Harold, sitting on the toilet lid, said it was "self-agitating." There is all manner of thrashing and screeching going on. Harold and Bell let this go on for about a minute or so to ensure that the cat is well-coated with the medication. At the appropriate time, in order to rinse the cat, Bell flushed the toilet three or four times.

Satisfied that the cat was sufficiently rinsed, Bell and Harold opened the top of the toilet. Sarah exploded from the toilet and disappeared somewhere into Becky's house. Bell said it is sort of nice that the mice got loose because now Sarah has a reward of sorts for having taken a bath. It was after Harold and Bell medicated the cat that the five gallons of paint and primer appeared.

The miracle of the engine was a whole different matter. The engine in the 6X was toast. It had a cracked block. There is no fixing that. What we needed was a whole new engine, and that would be major bucks that we didn't have and that we had no hope of raising. Bradley mentioned that there was an old, unused 6x just sitting out at the county barn. It had been there forever and no one there cared about it at all. It wasn't used, and no one knew the state of the engine in that one. If it had a sound block and heads, it was better than the one we had.

All it took was a little recon to discover that the engine in the 6X at the county barn was in outstanding shape. It helped that Pearson actually worked at the county barn and had a key to the gate. On inspection, it was discovered that the reason the 6X wasn't being used was that the rest of the truck was a mess. It had a busted spring in rear end, and bed was rusted through. It was obvious that the county was never going to use this 6X again. It took a night of drinking beer on the banks of the Spring River, but eventually a solution emerged. Before dawn, there was a detailed plan.

One of our other members, Custer, no relation the late General of Little Big Horn fame, worked at a sign company with access to a truck that had a small crane. On a Friday night, Custer "borrowed" the crane truck. Using the crane,

Bradley and Pearson pulled the engine from our 6X. On Saturday morning, Pearson and Bradley went to the county barn and prepared the engine in that 6X to be pulled. At the appointed time, Pearson opened the gate. Custer and another guy drove the crane truck carrying the old engine into the yard. They swapped engines with the county 6x and drove out with the "new" engine dangling from the crane. The entire operation took only about an hour and a half. By dark that evening, they had the "new" engine in our 6X and had made a test drive around the block in our newly functional army truck.

While Harold was solving the paint problem and Pearson and Bradley were solving the engine problem, the rest of us engaged in all sorts of stuff to raise money for the unit. We had a car wash once, and we'll never do that again. We worked like dogs. Because many of our members were hunters and hunters get their trucks really, really dirty, everyone brought their trucks to be washed. Those guys were perfectionists, and our car washing enterprise turned into an all-day detailing of beat-up trucks. About fifteen of us worked all day and we made about $35. Yep, that's not happening again.

A circus came to town and Mr. Grimmet swung a deal for us to direct traffic to park cars. That was a lot of fun, and we made $200 and didn't cause any wrecks.

The weirdest thing we did was scatter some dead guy's ashes over Craighead Lake. This wasn't our most successful endeavor. A guy called Bobcat had joined The Unit and he had just got his pilot's license. I don't know why we called him Bobcat, but we did. I, personally, think he joined The Unit because he was sweet on Becky. His dad owned the local TV station and also had a Cessna 182 airplane. That was the plane Bobcat had learned to fly in. The plan was for Bobcat and a helper to fly over Craighead Lake and dangle a paper bag with the guy's ashes out of the door. The wind would tear the bag, releasing the ashes over the lake while the guy's family watched from below. They were going to get $125 for doing that, and it sounded like it would be a piece of cake to do.

Well, on the day they were going to do it, a family member and the funeral director met Bobcat and his assistant at the airport. Bobcat, who as you know, was sweet on Becky. He had lured her there with the prospect of going flying. She had no idea about the scattering of ashes. We now knew the guy, whose ashes were in the bag, as Uncle Arthur.

The funeral director and family member had Uncle Arthur's ashes in a brown paper sack, and there were a bunch of slits cut in the sack. The odd ash or two escaped even just holding the bag. The funeral director was very solemn. He said that the slits in the bag would allow the wind to tear the bag at the right time and scatter Uncle Arthur's ashes, as planned, across the lake. The bag was attached to a twenty-foot piece, of what looked like, clothesline string. The plan was for Becky to hold the guy's ashes in her lap while they flew to the lake. It was very clear from the start that Becky was less than comfortable with this idea. She was very adamant about it. She really didn't want any part of holding some random guy's ashes, but Bobcat reasoned with her. In the end, Becky, being the trooper that she was, agreed to not only hold the ashes on the way to the lake, but also to deploy them out of the plane when the time came. Becky might have been a little sweet on Bobcat, too.

Becky and Bobcat took off right on time without any problems. Becky was sitting in the co-pilot seat and Bobcat was flying the plane. Craighead Lake isn't far from Jonbur, so they climbed to about 2500 feet and flew directly to the lake. Becky was very uncomfortable, but she hung in there. She had Uncle Arthur's ashes leaking out of the bag on her lap and was managing the creepiness of it very well. The family of the deceased were gathered at an open spot right by the lake. The spot actually was where the go-cart track used to be. The old track had the best overall view of the small lake.

As they approached the lake, Bobcat descended. He made the first pass low over the family and wiggled the wings to let them know it was him so they could get ready with cameras and stuff.

On the second pass, they were even lower, maybe fifty-feet off the water. Becky was holding the sack with the ashes, as if it were the clean end of a turd. The plan was that Bobcat would cut the motor back so that they would silently glide past the lake, losing a little altitude. Becky would push the door open just a bit with her shoulder so that she could let the wind take the sack out and let it trail behind the plane. The wind would tear the bag so that the ashes would get deposited over the lake. The timing of this was critical because it was important for the family to see the cloud of ashes come out behind the plane while it was over the lake.

It sounds like a simple plan. It was a simple plan. Simple things tend to blow up simple plans.

Turns out that the door was a little tricky to get open when flying because of the wind rushing by. When Becky pushed against it, the wind pushed back. The door didn't budge. She had to push really hard against the door, and still the wind pressed it closed. It wouldn't open. She pulled back some and hit the door with her shoulder really hard. This overcame the force of the wind holding the door shut. Then suddenly the door sprung open much wider than she had expected. With all her momentum going toward the door, even though she was secured in the plane by her seat belt, she felt as she were about to fall out of the plane. As any normal person would do when about to fall out of an airplane, she turned loose of the bag of ashes and desperately grabbed for a handhold. It is a perfectly normal and reasonable thing to do.

The bag, now loose in the cockpit, was caught by the sudden blast of whirling wind. It flew around the inside of the plane like a bat, releasing a dense, choking, cloud of ash. The result is a blinding fog of Uncle Arthur inside the cockpit of the plane.

This caught both Bobcat and Becky by surprise.

The family. watching from the go-cart track, stood motionless and silent as Bobcat and Becky silently glided in what appeared to be a burning airplane trailed by a cloud of the Uncle Arthur's ashes. For all the world, it looked like they were about to crash.

Unbeknownst to the family and friends watching from the go-cart track, inside the plane a desperate struggle for life was unfolding. Becky was skeeved out beyond comprehension. She was absolutely losing her mind. Bobcat added power to the plane and attempted to gently gain altitude. He struggled to fly the plane and to keep Becky from jumping out at the same time. To say Becky was traumatized is an understatement of galactic proportions. You simply cannot describe how creepy and gross it is to be engulfed by a swirling, blinding, choking, cloud of human ash and not be able to remove yourself from it. Becky was beside herself. It was quite a testament to Bobcat's flying skills that they did not crash into the lake while he was restraining Becky from leaping out of the plane.

JD and I were at the airport, completely unaware of any of this. We noticed that Bobcat's landing was more than a little rough. The plane bounced pretty high twice before settling down and rolling down the runway like you would expect. JD commented that Bobcat ought to practice landing a little more. However, we soon discovered that Bobcat was flying with one eye, because the other was completely blinded by ash. He was also flying the plane with one hand, because he needed the other to restrain Becky. She was still trying to jump out of the plane. When the Bobcat taxied up to us on the tarmac, there was still quite a bit of ash inside the plane. We could see there was a tremendous amount of activity in the plane. It looked like Becky was fighting a swarm of bees. As soon as it was possible and perhaps before the plane came to a complete halt, Becky burst from the plane coughing, screaming and looking like she just climbed out of a flour mill. She took off across the tarmac like a rabid raccoon. She was raising holy hell, brushing herself off madly and violently fluffing her long, brown hair. She was trailing an ever so faint haze of ash, as she ran across the tarmac. She was not happy. She was not happy at all. She was covered in the ashes of some poor dead bastard and had just endured a very rough landing with a one-eyed pilot. Beck was not a happy camper. I suspect that she isn't sweet on Bobcat anymore and I would bet good money that she will never fly again.

Uncle Arthur's relatives looked at Becky running and screaming down the tarmac, then at Bobcat who was squinting, one eye closed and covered with ash. The plane was still releasing a little bit of an ash cloud. The relative looked at the funeral director in utter horror. The funeral director, very calmly looked at Becky, as she reached the end of the tarmac and ran screaming across a field. Beck was not known for cussing, but on this day, she made up for it. You could still hear her halfway across the field. Finally, the funeral director looked at Bobcat, who was standing by the plane, still brushing Uncle Arthur's ashes off of himself.

The funeral director guy smiled.

"Good job!" he said, acting as if all this were normal. He presented us with a check. He began to calm the relatives down as he guided them back to the Cadillac. They climbed into the black Cadillac and they left.

As you can see, things ended fairly well. I remember thinking that I might have been living my best life. I was living on the farm, so I was free as a bird. It was fall but not yet winter. This meant that it wasn't screaming hot anymore and my workload was way down. School had started and I was getting there on time every day and doing fine. I was in a cool search and rescue unit. I hadn't been in any trouble at all for a long time and Mom was happy. Best of all, Dezi and I were back together.

Homecoming

Years ago, when that big bastard snatched me at the carnival and was about to kill me, Elvis had come to my rescue. In the pasture behind Elvis' house that night, he and the big bastard fought the most epic fight I have ever seen. Elvis might be a movie star, but he's tougher than a sack of nails, and he fights like Bruce Lee. After Elvis kicked his ass, the big bastard tried to get away, but The Goob hit him across the shins with an ax handle and then cold cocked him right across the eyes with it. The cops got the big bastard and Elvis took me and The Goob home. He met Mom and Dad that night. Ever since then, every Christmas I get a card and a gift from Elvis. He always sends Mom a birthday card and me an invitation to his birthday party. He and Mom were born on the same day.

When I got the invitation this year, it came to the farm. It hadn't been forwarded from the house. It was addressed to me at the farm. For just a second, I wondered how Elvis knew that I was at the farm. That thought passed right out of my brain when it occurred to me that this year, I should go to the party. Let me correct that, Dezi and I should go to the party. If you can take your girlfriend to meet the King of Rock and Roll, you should take your girlfriend to meet the King of Rock and Roll.

To get to the party, I had to survive Thanksgiving, Christmas, and New Year's, at Mom and Dad's house without some major event blowing everything up. I made a point of not going hunting on any of those days. Actually, because I lived north of town, I had cut way back on my duck hunting business. I went to Mom and Dad's house for Thanksgiving, but visited at Dezi's a little while too. Her parents were very nice. Her mother told me I needed a haircut again.

Christmas was a special event all its own. On Christmas Eve, Dad, Coachie, The Goob, and I, go quail hunting. We get a mess of quail that Mom fries up for dinner. Coachie is one of Dad's oldest friends and was Coach Harris's high school football coach back in Sweetwater, Mississippi. Dad and Coachie have been hunting together since before I was born.

I used to go hunting with Coachie a lot. We would bird hunt or duck hunt or deer hunt. Coachie was a great hunter. He taught me to call ducks. There's a lot more to duck calling than just blowing the call. You have to be able to read the ducks to know what to blow next. Coachie always had a great place to hunt. It wasn't too long ago that I realized something interesting. When we went bird hunting, what we really did was drive out in the hills until Coachie saw a spot that looked right. Then, we would park and hunt. Neither one of us had any idea whose land we were hunting. I think that's pretty funny now.

Every year Coachie says there aren't as many quail now as there used to be. He is right. Now, sometimes we don't get enough quail from the hunt. We have to get some from the quail farm to have a proper mess of quail. I'm always sad when we have to do that.

At some point in the afternoon on Christmas Eve, Mom asks me to go pick up Ralph. Ralph is Mom's helper. Ralph is about eighty years old now, honestly, he doesn't help much at all. He mostly sits at the end of the counter and visits with everyone. It's not Christmas Eve without Ralph.

When I go to pick up Ralph, I always park in his driveway and walk up to the house. I go up the front door and ring the doorbell. A casual glance around shows a home that is aged, but clean as a hound's tooth, usually freshly painted and very well-maintained. Ralph has his house painted every year.

He comes to the door in his tuxedo. He's only about five-and-a-half feet tall, but he walks like is the lord of the manor. His hair would be the envy of James Brown. He calls to Florida, his wife, to let her know he is leaving for his engagement. Then Ralph walks to the car as if he is walking in a coronation. Every time, the very first thing he does when he gets in the car is smile right at me and say how nice it is to see me again. I suspect that Ralph says that to everyone he meets. Each time he says it, he means it from the bottom of his heart. Ralph is a good Christian and gentle man.

With Ralph holding court at the end of the counter, Mom, Sweet Pea, Miss Dot, and Coachie, all go to work preparing dinner. Occasionally, I check on Ralph to see if he needs a drink or anything. Ralph doesn't drink alcohol, but he enjoys sweet tea. It's a circus of activity and a lively conversation is always conducted on topics ranging from Coachie and Miss Dot's latest travel adventure (Romania), to how much longer Bear Bryant was likely to coach at Alabama (only another year or two), to the unseasonably cold weather (it's gonna get worse before it gets better) we were having.

This year, I took this opportunity to talk to Dad some. I was really wanting to move back home. Riding the fences in the cold, blowing rain every day was starting to wear on me. I was tired of my cooking. I still didn't have a phone, so the only time I could talk to Dezi was when we were at school. He said he'd think about it and asked me to stay a few days at the house. I thought this was a good idea, but I suspected that I was going to end up back at the farm.

Remember how I said that whenever Walt showed up, amazing opportunities arose? Well, Walt showed up late in the afternoon on about the third day I was at the house. He knew I was there because he saw my truck. Jack and Hazel, Walt's parents, had gone to St. Louis for New Years and Walt was home alone. As I have said before, any time Walt is home alone, there are opportunities.

Jack owned a showroom perfect, candy apple red, Mustang Mach One with a 429 Cobra-jet engine. Fewer than a thousand of these cars had been produced. This was his baby. This car was probably the fastest car in Jonbur in terms of top-in speed. Joe and Hazel didn't take that car to St. Louis. It was way too sporty with it's bucket seats to be comfortable on a drive that long. They took the Thunderbird, a much more luxurious ride. On this cold, cold afternoon with Walt standing in my room, the red monster Mustang sat idling in my driveway. We were going for a ride.

Understand that Jack, being of sound mind, had not left a key to the Mustang at the house when he left for St. Louis. He had no illusions about whether or not Walt would take the car out. He was absolutely certain that Walt would, so he took all of his keys with him. Again, Jack had not taken into account Walt's ingenuity. What Jack didn't count on was that Walt would call the Ford place and go pick up a duplicate key for himself. Jack had simply underestimated the Walt's ability to improvise. I had noticed that people often underestimate Walt. He's a hell of a lot smarter than most folks think.

Walt and I took off in the Mustang. I had never ridden in it before, so this was quite a treat. It still had that new car smell. The downside to the 429 Cobra-Jet in the Mustang was that it got horrible gas mileage. Gas was about $0.29 a gallon and it took about eight or ten dollars to fill it up again. Of course, because the Mustang was the only candy apple red Mustang in Jonbur, we had to leave town to drive it, otherwise any number of people would rat us out. We headed to Paragould. In Paragould we were safe.

Paragould is a town about twenty minutes north of Jonbur. It's in a wet county so if you have a fake ID or know someone, you can get in a bar and have some beer. We had neither a fake ID nor a friendly acquaintance, so on this night there would be no beer for us. We just cruised the streets some. Eventually we pulled through a Sonic and got a coke. Just to be sure neither of us spilled the coke in the car, we parked on the strip and sat on the hood talking while we drank the cokes.

It didn't take long for some locals to get curious about the new candy apple read rocket setting on the strip. A truck blasting Skynyrd music and sporting a cooler overflowing with beer pulled in, and a bunch of guys got out. At first sight, I thought they might be escaped mental patients. The leader of this circus was a guy they called Captain America. He reminded me of Clint Eastwood, but without the personality. His best buddy was Lockwood, the tall guy with a bad haircut. He seemed to be the one who actually called the shots. Captain America was focused on the car, while Lockwood started the socializing. He called to the short guy, Da Greek, and had him get us a beer.. 'Da Greek' tossed us beers and was the first to greet us. The guy with muscles on top of muscles was Carmen. Carmen was a really nice guy and could have probably bench pressed the back of the Mustang. The Big Wop was the last of them. Apparently, Da Greek had pissed him off because about the only thing he ever said was "I hate you guys."

In five minutes, we were like best friends. Walt told them all about the car, and everyone got a chance to sit in the driver's seat. Da Greek wanted to drive it, but Walt said that might be a bad idea. I suspect this was one of the better decisions Walt made that night. Everybody, except for the Big Wop, talked and drank beer for a while. The Big Wop was still pissed at Da Greek. Eventually, Lockwood, whom Da Greek and Carmen called "Douchbag," asked us to join them on a trip to Tilly's.

Neither Walt nor I had heard of Tilly's. Douchbag explained that Tilly's was a strip club in the bootheel of Missouri. All you need to get in is either a Missouri ID showing you are over eighteen, or an out of state ID showing any age. They just didn't care about out of state folks of any age going in. Though none of us were eighteen, we all, Douchbag casually observed, had Arkansas IDs. We'd get in no problem.

Walt and I thought this over carefully. The bootheel wasn't real far, only about twenty-five miles from where we sat. We had plenty of gas. I had about fifty dollars, so we were okay money wise. Try as we might, neither of us could come up with a downside for this adventure. It seemed like a really good idea. Fifty bucks and an out-of-state strip club filled with naked girls! What could possibly go wrong? It was far enough from Jonbur that we didn't have to worry about running into someone we knew. The roads were good between here and there. If there was a problem, as long as we could get to the car, there wasn't a car around that could catch us. All we had to do was not get in a fight or get beat up. With Carmen with us, we didn't have to worry about that at all. There just wasn't a downside. Me and Walt were all in for the Missouri strip club.

On the way to Tilly's Walt and I caught up a lot. I hadn't seen much of Walt in the last year or so. Living on the farm really isolates you. I told Walt all about being in The Unit and how much fun that was. Walt wasn't into the outdoor adventure kind of thing. He was really into football and music, so he lifted weights a lot and went to a lot of concerts. It wasn't too long before we arrived at Tilly's.

Tilly's was set on a highway out in the middle of nowhere. There was nothing else around. I mentioned this to Douchbag when we all were gathered in the parking lot. Douchbag said it was out here so the law would leave them alone. There were only about a half dozen cars in the gravel parking lot. Douchbag said it was good we were early. The place will be packed in about an hour. I suspected that this wasn't his first visit to Tilly's.

Inside Tilly's it was dark, smelled of cigarettes and beer. The music was blaring. For just a moment, I had a flash back to the Dixie Chicken Gentleman's Club in Memphis. I guess all strip joints sort of have the same vibe to them. I looked around the room pretending to myself that I wasn't scanning for the big bastard, but in my heart, I knew I was. Once complete, I brushed it off. All that was a long time ago, I told myself. There were about a dozen guys around a couple of tables and they were having a hell of a good time. It was someone's bachelor's party, and they were making this count.

We found a table, and everyone ordered beer. It wasn't long until the show began, and what a show it was. Walt had never been to a strip club before. Back when the big bastard had been chasing me, I got a good look at the Dixie Chicken Gentleman's Club. I had even been in the dressing room. I knew what to expect, but Walt was rendered speechless. I don't think he was breathing for a while. One of the girls quickly eyed Carmen and led him away. She looked like a kid on Christmas Eve and she was about to open a gift. More guys drifted in from the parking lot.

The guys having the bachelor's party sent the groom into a special room with one of the girls. He was going to get something called a "lap dance." I wasn't sure what that was, but I suspected that it was going to be a lot of fun. A different group of dancers appeared on the stage. There were about four of them, and they all were very pretty, very shapely, and barely dressed. They were barely wearing any clothes at all. They brought two big poles out. They were shiny brass poles that anchored to the floor and to the ceiling. "They must be pole dancers," I thought. This is going to be fun. Even more guys found seats in the club as the room began to fill. The girls called for a volunteer.

Every hand in the room went up. Every guy in the place was like a dog on adoption day at the pound. Walt was beside himself. Having a second to think about this, I took my hand down. Something told me this was not a good idea. I told Walt to take his hand down but it was too late. We had been spotted. The girls wandered the room teasing each guy there just a little, then rejecting each outright. At each rejection, the rest of the guys howled with laughter and playfully heckled the rejected young reject just a little. One of the girls, a tallish girl with long brown hair approached me. She carefully looked me over as if she were looking at a piece of meat.

I had to take a couple of breaths. I hadn't seen this much of a woman since that night at the Dixie Chicken. The girls at the Dixie Chicken had saved my life, so I suspected that despite the nature of the job, this very pretty girl was likely just a nice girl making a living in a tough way. I looked closely at her. She was barely dressed, and her assets were readily apparent. You know how you get a vibe about a person? I got the vibe that this girl wasn't here because she was down and out, needing the job. Her vibe was of bucks, big bucks. I don't know why, but I could sense that this girl was rich. Despite the dramatic-and-bold eye makeup, this girl was not just your average stripper. She was somebody and she knew it. Maybe she was investing wisely.

While all this was going through my mind, I think she sensed my thoughts because she teased me with her riding crop for just a second. She leaned closely to my ear and softly whispered, "Maybe next time, Mr. Blue Eyes." Her perfume lingered in my nose. It wasn't the cheap perfume of the Dixie Chicken girls. It was a scent that dripped with money. She smiled at me, gave me a wink and a thumbs down. The crowd roared with laughter and taunted me a little bit. It was all good fun.

She moved on to Walt. With her a riding crop in her hand, She looked Walt over as if inspecting a stud horse. Using her riding crop, she lifted a bang of hair from Walt's eyes. He was focused on her like a laser beam. Timing her move with the end of the song that was playing, she tagged Walt on the head with the riding crop. He was the one.

It was almost like when they change acts at the circus! People were going everywhere. The audience was going wild with cheers and laughter as Walt was led up to the stage. Walt is a big guy. He was all-state tight end last year. They led him to the center of the stage. The music started again, and the lights were doing a synchronized thing to the beat of the music. With Walt standing in the center of the stage, they all began to dance around him, rubbing up against him in some very suggestive ways. Walt was soaking it up, grinning from ear to ear. The tall, brown-haired girl danced in front of him. She rubbed against him and fluffed his hair with her hands. Walt's eyes were locked on her. Even from my seat at the table, I could see that he was already sweating, sweating a lot. I think he had stopped breathing again. He does that sometimes, forgets to breath. The two other girls approached him from each side. He didn't even notice them. He was focused on the brown-haired girl. Everyone in the place was watching the brown-haired girl in front of him. She was the star.

Suddenly, Walt had a cuff on each wrist. The cuffs were attached to ropes that led to the top of each pole. He noticed the cuffs. He looked at them for a second, not realizing what was about to happen. The girls hauled down on the ropes and Walt's arms were stretched out to either side as far as they could go. He was trapped. We howled. Walt wasn't amused, but the rest of the room sure as hell was.

The girls came back to him, dancing, teasing him. He struggled mightily. Walt's pretty strong, but this night, Walt was trapped. The teasing went on for a little while, then it began to escalate. The brown-haired girl approached him. Using scissors, she cut his shirt so that she could raise it up over his head and tie it. Though he was breathing out of an arm hole, he was now effectively blindfolded. He could not see a thing. By this time, Walt knew he was in serious trouble. Walt was giving it everything he had, but there was no escape. The poles held fast.

Feathers were next. The girls unmercifully tormented him with long ostrich feathers. Walt is very ticklish. There were times when he was turning blue. They might relent for a minute to let him breath, and then get him again. This continued for about ten minutes. The guys and I were drinking beer like mad. Mostly naked women torturing the hell out of Walt really is the greatest show ever.

The two girls, who had secured Walt's wrists, approached him slowly from either side. Each had something in hand, but it was too small to see. While they had everyone's attention, the brown-haired one slipped behind Walt. Walt seemed to be focused on the two girls. They were saying something to him. Walt was starting to panic. Just as he was struggling as if there were no tomorrow, the brown-haired girl got him from behind with a cat-o-nine tails. That is a whip thing that you use to lash someone. She really laid into him. The brown-haired girl was wearing him out with that thing.

Walt howled and fought madly against the restraints. The girls, to either side, did something to his nipples. Walt screamed. The guys and I were losing out minds. The girls stepped back and we could see that Walt appeared to have Tilly's Christmas tree ornaments dangling from his nipples. They had red-and-white blinking lights and had little jingle bell things on them. Walt was fighting like hell to get loose. The brown-haired girl was really laying into him with the cat-o-nine tails, and with each move you could hear the jingle bells ring. It beat all I have ever seen. Douchbag, Da Greek, Captain America, and I, laughed so hard that no one couldn't breathe. I thought I was dying.

Just then the doors burst open and cops started pouring in. People scattered everywhere. It instantly became a madhouse. With the strobe lights still flashing, and the music still blaring, the girls disappeared through the stage door. I dashed to the stage, and using my knife, cut the ropes that held Walt. Walt was free. He ripped what was left of his shirt from his head. We were dashing out through the fire exit where a deputy almost got us. The deputy was waiting outside of the fire escape just in case someone tried to escape the raid that way. Walt ran over him like a turtle in the road. If you are supposed to secure a door, you need to be big enough to not get run over when someone runs out of the door. Running across the dark parking lot, the red-and-white lights flashing from the Christmas tree ornaments dangling from Walt's nipples were a lot brighter than they had been inside. They lit up the night. Walt used his hands to keep the ornaments from bouncing and tearing at his nipples, but the jingle bells made noise anyway. Aside from police hollering orders inside the club, jingle, jingle, jingle was the only noise we heard as we ran across the parking lot to the car.

In three seconds, we were in the Mustang and the engine roared to life. Walt pulled the car down into first gear and stomped the accelerator. We pealed out of the parking slinging gravel every where. The engine screamed as Walt took it up through the gears to fourth gear and we began the sprint back to Arkansas. In four seconds, there were two or three Missouri State Police in hot pursuit. Despite being half blinded by the flashing lights from the Christmas tree ornaments, Walt pushed the Mustang almost to its redline as we fled back to Arkansas. I will just mention that the next time I go that fast, I would prefer to be in an airplane.

Every bump we hit caused Walt to cuss and the jingle bells to jingle. The Missouri State Police blue lights were barely visible in the rear view mirror as we crossed the state line into Arkansas. Because Walt had experience in these matters, we got off the highway right away. The Missouri cops will have radioed the Arkansas cops, and they would be coming to find us on the highway. Walt drove Jack's Mustang down some muddy gravel roads for a while to avoid any Arkansas police that the Missouri cops might have alerted. This was a painful route for Walt, but it was the right one to take. It was clear to me that it would be hard to miss a candy apple red Mustang Mach One containing two men, one of whom had flashing red-and-white Christmas tree ornaments attached to his nipples. While we were going down the gravel roads, I tried to get the ornaments off the nipple rings. While I was trying to do this, we hit a bump. Walt screamed and hit me over the head. Seems the bump had caused me to tug the Christmas tree ornament in a most painful way. I figured we would just have to wait until we got somewhere that we could stop. I cautioned Walt about the trees. I sure didn't want a repeat of the whole golf cart thing. Walt slowed down a lot.

We eventually and uneventfully made it back to Jonbur and took Jack's Mustang to a car wash. Right after I got the ornaments off of Walt's nipple rings, we cleaned the car up until it looked showroom perfect. We carefully inspected the car to make sure that all traces of it having been driven on gravel had been removed by the wash.

In the light of the car wash, I was able to see Walt clearly for the first time. His shirt, of course, was in shreds from the strip club. Remembering the incident with the shoes, I asked, "That wasn't Little Jack's shirt was it?"

Walt just looked at me. His bare torso was streaked with red whelps where the brown-haired girl had flogged him with the cat-o-nine tails. He looked terrible front and back. The streaks were so bad that it was easy to miss the nipple rings. Finally, he said, "Yeah, it was." He looked at me and said, "It was his Kappa Alpha Old South T shirt."

Why was I not surprised?

Finally, I looked at his nipples. His nipples had seen better days. Each nipple was pierced with a ring, and the strippers had hung a Christmas ornament from each ring. I held the ornaments in my hand. If you looked closely at the charm, you could see that it said "Tilly's." I suspected that Tilly's had been selling Christmas ornaments during the holiday season. Who buys a Christmas tree ornament from a strip club? I turned the lights off on the ornaments and put them in my pocket. I was keeping these. I had to use wire cutters to get the nipple rings off Walt. He hollered as I cut each one, but I got them off. His nipples were bleeding some and were pretty sore. I told him to go get a tetanus shot.

"Wouldn't you hate to get lockjaw from an infected nipple? How would you like to explain that?" I asked. In my head, I resolved to never again do anything I would not want to explain to the ER doctor.

For Walt, it had been a tough night. He was sporting two pierced nipples and had been thrashed with a cat-o-nine tails. When you think about it, we had made it through without any serious damage to anything except Walt's nipples. Jack's Mustang was clean as a whistle and back in the garage undamaged. I call that a win.

There was one more holiday I had to survive before Elvis' birthday party. On New Year's Eve there was always a good party at Mr. Minnot's house. Mr. Minnot was old farm money, and half the town thought he was gay. He had never married and always seemed to have a pretty, young "niece" on his arm. Every year he had a huge New Year's party that everyone in town wanted to go to. Mom and Dad were invited because he knew Dad from way back. I got invited because he was one of my duck hunting clients. Mr. Minnot enjoyed duck hunting, cigars, and good bourbon. He always brought his own and was kind enough to share with me. He was a history nut, so we had a lot in common. I invited Dezi to go to the party with me. If Dezi was there, I could be reasonably sure that everything would be all right.

New Year's Eve was a cold night with the remnants of a snow fall remaining on the lawns. Mr. Minnot lived in one of the huge old mansions on Main Street. The house had been in his family for over a hundred years and sat on three acres in the middle of town. It had a twelve-foot-tall masonry wall all around it.

On entering the home, you are immediately impressed by the huge staircase in the foyer. Neither Dezi nor I had ever seen the inside of the house before, so we were just dumb struck at the sheer size of everything. The foyer alone could probably hold fifty people. It was about the size of the foyer in *The Sound of Music*. To the left was the bar room, and to the right was the music room. Everything was a dark wood, and the ceilings were about fifteen feet high. After exploring this amazing home for a bit, Dezi thought it would be proper to go and say 'hi' to our host, Mr. Minnot. First, before we did that, she had to go to the ladies room.

When she returned, I spotted Mr. Minnot across the way in the bar room. He was engaged in a lively conversation with Mayor Wilkens. Just then, a very pretty young lady walked up and took his arm. She would absolutely give that old man a heart attack, I thought to myself. We waited our turn to greet Mr. Minnot.

"Mr. Minnot, how are you this evening?" I said as I extended my hand. We shook hands and I introduced Dezi to him. Mr. Minnot is a very gracious man who just oozed southern grace and charm. Though educated at Princeton in the 1950s, he retained a very relaxed southern drawl. He greeted Dezi warmly then he introduced the pretty young lady on his arm. "This is my niece, Victoria," he said.

I looked at Victoria as we were introduced. I felt like I had met her before, She was beautiful in her gown and she had her hair up. Her makeup was classically understated and was very nicely done. It merely accentuated the beauty that nature had given this woman. She smiled broadly and greeted Dezi first. As she turned to me to shake my hand, her eyes twinkled as if she were suppressing a laugh. I caught a whiff of perfume just before she spoke. I knew that perfume. My brain began to spin. That was expensive perfume. I suddenly became very dizzy. It was the perfume that I first smelled at Tilly's. Victoria smiled as she said, "Well, how are you tonight, Mr. Blue Eyes."

I froze.

I tried to make polite conversation, but it was useless. I couldn't think. This was the brown-haired girl from Tilly's. My mind was spinning, and Victoria could tell that it was. She was enjoying this immensely. Every other sentence she managed to work in a discrete reference or mention something that was reminiscent of the other night at Tilly's. I was beyond a nervous wreck. My brain was in overdrive. I wondered if Mr. Minnot knew his niece was a stripper at Tilly's? Should I tell him? How could I tell him without admitting I was there? I had a thousand questions and fears bouncing off the sides of my brain when Dezi finished the polite conversation and we walked away.

"I hope you know," Dezi began, "Mr. Minnot's niece is not his niece."

"Really?" I said, acting like I wasn't surprised.

"And Mr. Minnot isn't gay either," she added with a huge smile.

"How do you know that?" I continued wondering if she could have somehow picked up on all the hidden references that Victoria had been dropping in the conversation. My heart rate had to be 150, and there is no telling what my blood pressure was. I was sweating and starting to hyperventilate.

"She told me. I met her in the ladies room when we got here. She's very nice," she said. Struggling to hold back a laugh, Dezi continued, "She saw us when we came in and recognized you. She said you met the other night at Tilly's."

I was stuck. I didn't know what to say.

Dezi laughed and continued, "I know it's a strip club up in the bootheel, silly. She said she was going to torment you some for fun." Dezi, smiling like mad, broke into a good laugh. She found all this incredibly funny.

Me, not so much.

"Did she really hang Christmas tree ornaments off someone's nipples?" she laughed.

"Yes," I said. "They had flashing red-and-white lights on them, and little jingle bells."

"Were they your nipples?" Dezi's asked and her eyes sparkled as she laughed. She was dying to know.

"No, they were Walt's nipples," I told her. "He says they are still pretty sore."

"I have to see them," she laughed.

A Birthday Party

Elvis's birthday is Jan 8th but the 8th was on a Thursday. Elvis planned his party for that Saturday evening. Mom's birthday is on January 6th. I went by Mom and Dad's to take Mom a birthday gift on her birthday. I kind of surprised her but she was glad to see me. I noticed that her eye didn't twitch anymore. She seemed very relaxed. I think she actually was relaxed. I felt good about that. I think me living at the farm had helped out a lot. It didn't hurt that she and Dad really liked Dezi.

Our plan for the date was pretty simple. Elvis' party was supposed to start at about five o'clock. Dezi and I, in my sparkling-clean, pink 1967 Caddy, would leave Jonbur at about noon. Memphis is only about an hour-and-a-half from Jonbur, but I didn't want to take any chances with being late. Even if there was a wreck on the bridge over the Mississippi River, we would still have plenty of time. My thinking was that we could swing by Overton Square, visit TGI Fridays for a snack and goof off some. We would still have plenty of time before we headed down into Whitehaven where Graceland was.

The trip over to Memphis went just as planned. No problems whatsoever. We cruised out of Jonbur on Highway 63. I was very careful through Bay and Truman to make sure that I did not speed. They will give you a ticket there in a heartbeat. For the ten miles before Payneway, the road ran beside a huge ditch. Legend has it that they got dirt out of the ditch to raise the road up so that when the crop lands flooded, the road would still be drivable. I don't know for sure, but I always thought that putting a deep ditch full of stagnant water beside the highway was a bad idea. What if you got run off the road or something?

Though cold, the day was a great day for a trip to Memphis. The sky and the road were both clean and clear. Dezi was understandably excited about meeting Elvis. Though not a big fan, she, like everyone else on earth, was captivated by his stage persona. I told him if she thought he seemed nice on stage, she was going to be blown away at how nice he was in person. We had a nice snack at TGI Friday. Their fries are the best. Then, just so we wouldn't be late, we headed to Whitehaven. We could go the Southland Mall or something there to kill time till the party. In that mall, they had a Spenser's Gifts! It is, you know, the world's greatest store.

Dezi and I got to Whitehaven about an hour-and-a-half before the party was supposed to start. As I drove past Graceland on the way to Southland Mall, the bright and flashing neon across the street from Graceland caught Dezi's eye. Dezi saw the sign over the Dixie Chicken Gentleman's Club. It was impossible to miss and hard to ignore.

"That's where it started?" she exclaimed, pointing to the club.

"Not exactly," I said. "It got started in the parking lot back there. There was a carnival that night," I continued as we drove down Elvis Presley Boulevard toward the Southland Mall. I really didn't want to talk about it. Most folks think that the story is just an exciting adventure, but to me it was reliving a nightmare.

"I want to see it," Dezi shouted practically bouncing up and down in her seat. Dezi wanted desperately to go see the place where it all happened. Reluctantly, I turned the car around and we went back to the little shopping center across from Graceland. I would rather quickly walk her through the story once than talk about it for the next hour-and-a-half. They say a picture is worth a thousand words, and if I could show her where it happened, I wouldn't have to talk about it as much. I could avoid the thousand questions. I parked sort of in the center of the parking lot so I could point and explain how the carnival was set up and she would be able to see where I ran to. I hoped to not get out of the car. Dezi was intent on seeing it all up close and in person, so we got out of the car and walked the lot.

As we looked at the club from the parking lot, I realized that the Dixie Chicken was a lot bigger and gaudier than I remembered. I really didn't get a good look at it that night, but this was a very different place now. When the big bastard chased me a cross the parking lot, I was focused on getting away. I really didn't look around a lot, and I didn't take in a lot of detail. I remember that when all this happened, I first tried to go in a grocery store. I remember that the door was locked. The grocery store isn't there anymore. Next, I tried to go into a barber shop. It was locked and it is gone now. It looked like the Dixie Chicken had expanded into their spaces.

Dezi asked me about what happened that night. I don't like to talk about it, but I told her about the big bastard yanking me out of the Scrambler and how that broke my ankle. We walked over by where the Scrambler had been set up. There is a 7-Eleven store near there now. She just looked for a minute or two at where the Scrambler had been set up. I told her about getting away from that big bastard by pinching that girl on the butt. She laughed about that but she didn't laugh at all when I told her about what it's like trying to hide in the narrow halls of a Haunted House. For just that moment, I could smell the smells I smelled that night. I remembered that the big bastard needed a shower and had recently eaten something with way too much garlic. I could smell it again. It gave me chills. Dezi asked me how I ran on a broken ankle all the way to the Dixie Chicken. I told her that it really didn't hurt much more than an ordinary sprained ankle.

We walked over to the front of the Dixie Chicken. The Club had all manner of neon lights on it now. I didn't remember it being so bright. I didn't even see the sign that said it was the Historic Dixie Chicken Gentleman's Club. What's historic about a strip club? There were some posters up with pictures of some really pretty girls who worked there. I went over to the front door of the place. I was surprised when I saw them. They were huge and on either side of the door. There was a poster with a photo of that big bastard in handcuffs. Another poster had a photo of me, Elvis, and The Goob, holding his ax handle. It looked like it had been taken by the barn the night of the fight. Dezi studied the poster for a few long minutes. I was looking forward to leaving. I thought that she had seen it all.

I was wrong. Dezi really, really, wanted to peek inside. I had a bad feeling about this. Kind of a feeling of impending doom, a rising fear.

"That's not a good idea," I said. I really just wanted to leave. "They used to have a couple of really big bouncers in there to throw you out. I don't want to get beat up before Elvis' party," I cautioned.

"Just a peek," Dezi said, as she opened the door just a bit. She stuck her head in. She looked around a little, then she slipped through the door disappeared into the darkness of the club. The door shut with the solid sound of solid wood.

It seemed like forever, but was probably only a minute or two later, her head pokes out. "You got to see this!!! You won't believe it!" she said excitedly as she grabbed my arm and dragged me into the entry of the club.

"Oh damn," I thought, "this is not good. Not good at all."

It was cold, and dark in the entryway to the club. Just like at Tilly's the other night, the smell of stale beer and cigarette smoke made it all come back to me. The walls were still painted black, and all of the hardware on the doors was still chrome. There were mirrors everywhere and the music was so loud you couldn't hear yourself think. I could feel panic starting to rise. I glanced around remembering in my mind the two bouncers lying dead on the floor. There was a fog coming off the stage. I looked up toward the stage halfway expecting to see a mostly-naked lady dancing with a midget and a snake. "Some things never change," I thought. I instinctively looked over to where the bouncers were sitting that night. Two big guys, bouncers, were in that same spot now, talking. They had not seen us yet. Again, I looked over where the two bouncers had laid the night the big bastard killed them. Now, there were white painted outlines on the floor where the two men had laid. I remembered they were laid out like cord wood. Except for Uncle Johnny, they were the first dead guys I had ever seen. Uncle Johnny wasn't bloody. These guys were pretty bloody. I looked over at the bar where the bar tender stood when he called the cops. In my mind, I could see him again. I didn't like this at all.

For the very first time, I noticed the counter. The counter was new. There was a cash register on the counter. The counter had a glass top and there were T-shirts and bandannas, autographed photos and all manner of junk for sale in there. Belt buckles. They even had Dixie Chicken Gentleman's Club belt buckles. Everything said, "Dixie Chicken Gentleman's Club." There were bumper stickers about the Historic Dixie Chicken. I paused when I saw that they were selling autographed photos of me and The Goob.

The autographed photos of the dead bouncers kind of caught me by surprise. Well, all that's new, I thought. The girl behind the counter frowned at me, smiled at Dezi, and pressed a button.

On the wall behind the counter there was what appeared to be a memorial. Dezi dragged me closer. There were dozens of photos and newspaper write ups all very tastefully framed in picture frames.

I stepped closer. Dezi pointed at one with a photo and said, "Is that you?" Sure enough, it was the photo from the interview the day I learned you could say "pecker" on the radio. I realized all these news stories and photographs were about the night I tried to hide from the big bastard here! They had photos of the two bouncers who he killed, and their whole life story. Apparently, they were just good ole boys, dead before their time. Before I could finish reading the first one, a giant hand grabbed me by the back of the neck and nearly lifted me off the floor. One of the bouncers, having been summoned by the buzzer rung by the girl at the counter, had me by the neck and was dragging me toward the door.

As another bouncer was about to grab Dezi, she screamed and kicked him in the gonads. The whole place came to a stop. The music even stopped. The bouncer froze in his steps and bent over. Dezi pointed at me and grabbed one of my autographed photos off the counter. She shouted at the bouncer who had me, as she pointed at that photo, "He's the kid in the picture!!! Look! Don't you get it?? It's him!!"

The bouncer who had me by the neck, stopped. He looked at the photo, and then at me. The other bouncer, still recovering from Dezi's kick to the gonads, straightened up. He looked at Dezi, then he looked at the other bouncer. He walked over to the photo and looked intently. He motioned to the bouncer who had me. We went over, and they both looked at the photo, and then at me. The bouncer that Dezi kicked cleared his throat and managed to say, "Call Eddie. He's gonna want to talk to this kid."

They dragged both of us into a little private room toward the back of the club. The room had a table, a stripper pole, and a really nice leather couch. It was closed off from the rest of the bar by thick, red velvet curtains. The lights were really low, and the music wasn't quite as loud.

"Sit there," the smaller bouncer growled above the music, pointing to the couch.

When we sat, we realized that the couch wasn't really leather. It was kind of gross because it was sticky. We waited, and waited, and waited. I watched the time creep by knowing that I really didn't want to be late to Elvis' birthday party.

Finally, the music stopped and the curtains parted and a couple of guys walked in. One of the guys had a neon-colored jogging suit on, but I'm sure he didn't jog much. He was the boss. One of the bouncers came over. He roughly reached in my back pocket and took my wallet. He protected his gonads and politely asked Dezi for her ID. He handed both IDs to the guy in the jogging suit. He looked at my driver's license and at Dezi's.

He looked at Dezi's for a minute. He did a double take and then, looking at Dezi, he said, "Desirable? Your name is Desirable?"

I was stunned. Looking at Dezi I said, "What?"

The guy looked at Dezi and said again, "Your name is Desirable?" Smiling, he looked her over top to bottom. With his eyes twinkling like the night sky, he enthusiastically added, "Well! Yes, you are!"

"Shut up," came the icy reply. "My name is Dezi." Just as Dezi snatched her ID back from the guy, one of the bouncers shouted, "Watch her! She'll kick you in the nuts."

The guy laughed a little, protected himself and said, "Dezi it is."

"Your name is Desirable?" I asked again.

"Shut up, Junior," she said as laser beams emerged from her eyes and I understood not to mention it again.

Touche. Well played, Dezi. Well played.

The guy looked at my ID. He looked at it for a minute, then he handed my license and wallet back to me. He smiled like he had just found a long-lost brother. He gave me a big hug and in a very solid New Jersey accent said, "Blondi! Welcome back! How ya been, kid?"

Dezi looked at me and asked, "Blondie? Your name is Blondie?"

"I'll explain later," I replied knowing that this was going to be payback for asking about her name.

Without waiting for an answer, he looked at the bouncer and said, "Danny, get the kids a beer."

Over the next thirty minutes or so, Eddie O'Hare, proud owner of the Dixie Chicken Gentleman's Club (and just about every other strip club for fifty miles around), told me about how the publicity from the fight and capturing the big bastard had made his club world famous. People, he said, came from all around the world to his club now. Mostly they were Elvis nuts and the occasional Elvis impersonator. They have their own wall of photos, he said. Most visitors didn't care anything about the strippers. They were interested in the story of what happened. He sold them expensive drinks and a lot of souvenirs. I mentioned the autographed photos. Eddie's expression changed some. He looked at me. He squinted at me and said in a slightly menacing voice, "So, um, you're not gonna want a cut of that action, are you?"

I assured him I didn't, but that I would like to have one of the photos. He smiled and his voice went back to the "Happy Eddie" voice. He looked at one of the bouncers and said, "No problem. Danny, get the kids one of each of the photos."

He showed Dezi and me all around. All over the place hung photos of famous people who had come here to see where it had happened. There were movie stars, and rock stars and politicians. Most of the politicians were from either Louisiana or France. It appears that having your picture up in a strip club isn't a bad thing for politicians from Louisiana or France. Eddie said the whole thing had made him a rich man. It was his big break and now he owned many strip clubs. He said he had me to thank for it. I think the fact that clubs that didn't belong to him tended to suffer fires probably contributed to his success some, too. But I didn't say so.

I asked if any of the ladies who helped me were still there. I wanted to thank them again for helping me. Eddie said, "Only one is still here." He said it's been about six or seven years and that most of the girls had moved on to other things now. That made me kind of sad because without them, that big bastard would have killed me right here on the spot.

Eddie told me about how badly the big bastard had beat up lady who was dressed as the nurse. Her courage inspired him, and he fell in love with her. They have been married for about four years now. Her name was Cynthia, and she was still a major draw for the club. She doesn't dance any more. Now she visits with guests and talks about the night it happened, poses for pictures and signs autographs. I guess there was a happy ending after all.

Eventually, we wound up in Eddie's office. It was very elegant, and tastefully decorated. It looked more like the office of a wealthy lawyer than the owner of a chain of strip clubs. Against one wall was a bourbon collection to die for. I thanked Eddie for the tour and told him that we had to go because Elvis' party would start soon and we shouldn't be late. Eddie took out a business card and wrote on the back of it. He told me I was welcome in any of his clubs at any time, just show the bouncer this card. The password is Flyboy. He also said that if I was ever in a jam and needed help, call the number on the back. I thanked him. Dezi and I turned to leave.

As we were leaving, Eddie said, almost in passing, "You know he's out now, don't you?"

Those words echoed across the office.

I froze.

I turned back to Eddie. I must have gone pale. What he said just couldn't mean what I knew it did. Dezi didn't understand what he had just said, but I sure as hell did. My face must have spoken volumes because, almost as if on cue, Eddie continued.

"The Tennessee Court of Appeals judge threw out the conviction. The judge said the man was beat up too badly for an eight-year-old boy to have done it. He said that the police had to have beat the hell out of the man," Eddie said. The big bastard, if you remember, was captured after The Goob skewered him through the ass with a pitchfork and whacked across the shins and eyes with an ax handle. The Goob was eight years old at the time, but he was a really big eight. He was my size at the time. The size of a ten-year-old. "The court set him free and said he can't be tried again. Something about double jeopardy. Hector Butterfield has been a free man for about three weeks now," Eddie continued.

In the thirty seconds that conversation took, every bit of fun the night had promised simply disappeared. Like dust in a summer breeze, the joy was gone as if it had never really been there at all. I had never even known the man's name until now. I'm sure I heard it at trial, but trial was mostly a blur. I just didn't remember much about the trial. I remember that big bastard saying that one day he would feed my liver to

the fish. Hector Butterfield. Just thinking the name made me
I feel sick.

Though I wanted to just go home, it was time for the
party. As we walked out of the Dixie Chicken in the early
winter darkness, across Elvis Presley Boulevard, the
Christmas lights of Graceland lit the night. Everything that
could be adorned with lights was adorned with lights. There
was a little manger scene deep in the yard, right in front of
the front door to the mansion. Though we were a week into
January, Elvis' house still looked like the night before
Christmas. Dezi and I both were struck by the sheer beauty of
it all. In the cold night air, our warm breath made clouds as
we stood and just took it all in. For a moment, and just a
moment, the big bastard left my mind again. I was standing
with Dezi taking in the beauty and serenity of a cold, winter
night in Memphis.

We drove across Elvis Presley Boulevard to enter
Graceland. The guard at the gate didn't want to let us in. No
one exercises more authority more than a solitary eighteen-
year-old kid manning a guard shack in front of Graceland on
Elvis' birthday. I had thought to bring the invitation with us. I
showed it to him. He wasn't impressed. He frowned at me,
pronounced it a fake, and still tried to turn us away. Finally,
and very reluctantly, he went in the little guard shack and

made a call up to the house. A moment later, without even looking at us, he opened the gate and waved us through. We drove up to the house. I parked beside another Cadillac, near some Lincolns and a weird, yellow Volkswagen with a gold grill on it like the grill on a Rolls Royce. There was a beat up truck with Texas tags on it over by the rose bushes. I knew whose truck that was.

Dezi was understandably excited as we approached the front door of the mansion. I told her that the house not as big as it looks, but she was already lost in the moment. The foyer was full of people milling about and talking. To the left was the dining room, and there was a great spread of food on the table. Dezi almost fainted when she saw Cher standing by Lee Majors. They were both in line for the shrimp. To the right of the foyer was the living room. It was crowded, too. The only person I recognized in there was Dave Brown, the Memphis weatherman. What in the hell was the weatherman doing at Elvis' birthday party? I saw Vern across the room, and when he saw us, he came right over. He gave me a big hug and talked about how much I had grown. With disapproval in his eye, he mentioned that I needed a haircut. I introduced Dezi to him. I told her about the summer of working in the garden and canning all the great things we grew. It was, I said, probably the best summer I ever had.

Vern was looking great. We talked about the days we spent in the garden, and I told him I lived on a farm now caring for Dad's cattle. He laughed about that because he knows how much work taking care of cattle was. Talking with Vern brightened me up some, and I was starting to push what Eddie had told me further into the back of my mind. After we had discussed about all you could discuss about gardens and cows, Vern saw Mac Davis across the room and waved him over.

Mac Davis seems about as country as you would expect. He's from Texas. Mac remembered me from Elvis' party a few years ago. Mac remarked about how much I had grown. He, too, said I needed a haircut. He asked me if I was in a band yet, and Dezi laughing, said, "Have you heard him sing?"

Mac laughed and Vern introduced him to Dezi. Vern asked Mac to entertain Dezi while he and I went to get us all something to drink. At the bar, I got a coke for Dezi and me. Vern looked at me cross ways about that for a second then asked for sweet tea. Vern only drinks black coffee or sweet tea. The sugar in soda pop rots your teeth, he says. He turned to me. "You know they done let that big bastard out of the penitentiary," he said in a very serious voice. "He was supposed to go to the chair, but he's out now. Some judge didn't believe The Goob beat him up so bad," he continued.

"I heard," I said without telling him how I had heard. Vern would never approve of a strip joint being right across the street from his home. He certainly would not approve of me and Dezi hanging out there with Eddie and Cynthia.

As this was soaking in, I sensed someone staring at me. For just a second, that old fear was crawling up my back. With panic rising, quickly I looked around everywhere. Then, a movement across the room caught my eye. I looked up, and a huge man was coming. He parted the crowd of rock stars and groupies like Moses parted the Red Sea. My heart stopped. How could this be? Could this day get any worse? I looked over at Dezi. She saw the man coming through the crowd, too. I glanced around for an escape, but I was boxed in. Dezi realized what was going on. She ditched Mac Davis and cut through the crowd like a shark. Mac, being a gentleman and sensing something was amiss, closely followed her over.

The giant man crashed over me like a tidal wave breaking against the boulders on a rocky shore. Laughing like a man out of his mind, he put me in a head lock and gave me a good knuckle brushing on the top of my head. As I desperately fought to escape, he suddenly turned me loose.

He spun me around, gave me a huge hug and slapped me on the shoulders. Smiling as big as Dallas, he said, "Kid! Good to see you again!" as if I were his long-lost best friend. Dezi arrived and was about to kick him in the gonads, but I stopped her.

"It's okay," I said urgently, as I stepped between Dezi and the man. "Dezi, this is Jerry Lawler!"

Still smiling from ear-to-ear, Jerry Lawler greeted Dezi warmly. He then turned to Vern and said, "Vern, how do you know the kid here?"

Mr. Lawler had never heard the story about how the big bastard had robbed a bank down at Walls and kidnapped me. Vern does a good job telling the story. It gets better each time he tells it. The Goob is going to need a cape someday if it gets any better. Mr. Lawler laughed as hard as anyone I have ever heard when Vern told him about how I escaped from the big bastard by using the sheriff's throw-down gun to shoot through the seat of the car and shot the man's penis off. Dezi, hearing some of this for the first time, was shocked. I hadn't told her all the details that Vern relished in recounting. When we got to the part about the carnival and the night my ankle was broken, Mr. Lawler didn't laugh at all until the part when The Goob got the big bastard in the ass with the pitchfork.

When Vern told about Elvis fighting the big bastard, Mr. Lawler was really tuned in to every punch and kick as Vern described the fight. When the big bastard tried to make a getaway but got stopped when The Goob whacked him across the shins with the ax handle, Mr. Lawler laughed so hard I thought he was going to fall out. He said he wanted to meet "that kid, The Goop."

"The Goob," I blurted out before I realized it. A wise man doesn't correct a professional wrestler.

"I've heard it both ways," he said smiling at me and winking at Dezi. Mr. Lawler is a guy that is really easy to like. He took a second or two to compose himself after laughing so hard. Suddenly, he turned back to Vern.

"So, this is a for real southern fairy tale," Mr Lawler said, "because it starts with 'You ain't going to believe this shit.'" And then he started to tell the story of how Walt and I destroyed the convertible top on his prized Cadillac one night at the Country Club. Mr. Lawler, being a somewhat larger than life man, and a very loud speaker by nature, captured the attention of everyone at the party as he told the story. The whole thing, he said, started with his need to find a secluded spot for an amorous engagement. According to Mr. Lawler, when Walt and I began our dash up the hood of his car, it scared his date so bad she nearly bit his tongue off. When we crashed right though the convertible top, it scared the crap out of him. One minute he is just about to get lucky and the next minute one of us landed a foot right square of his back. He said it knocked the wind out of him, but I don't think so.

If I remember correctly, he was doing a lot of cussing the whole time we were trying to escape. I don't think he missed a breath at all. He said he had a bruise in the shape of a size nine tennis shoe in the small of his back for weeks. Everyone laughed loudly as he told the story. His description of the chase through the trees had people on the floor dying. He painted a hilarious portrait of a souped-up Cadillac chasing a pimped-out golf cart with two screaming boys on it through the trees on a golf course. It was just too much for most people. Many were gasping for air as Mr. Lawler milked the story for every laugh. As he told the story, he held his hands up as if he were steering a car. He used exaggerated body motions to simulate dodging in and out of trees as he dashed in and out of the crowd as he simulated the chase. When he got to the part about me and Walt wrecking the cart, people were laughing so hard they were turning blue. I didn't know that he and his date had watched the tree burn while the tow truck pulled his Cadillac out of the sand trap. He finished the story by telling everyone how Walt and I had paid to repair his Cadillac and to replace Walt's father's golf cart.

He put his huge gorilla arm around me like an old friend as he spoke. I felt like he was actually proud of me and Walt. Again, Dezi was somewhat taken aback. She had never heard the golf cart story from that perspective. Mr. Lawler does a great job telling it. I don't think anyone enjoys telling a story more than Mr. Lawler.

After the he finished telling the story, Elvis came over smiling and laughing. You could tell he had been laughing his butt off. I introduced him to Dezi. For just a second, Dezi was like a frozen duck. She didn't move, blink, or speak. She might have been in brain lock. Just a few words from Elvis broke the ice though. Pretty soon they were chatting like old friends. While Elvis and Dezi engaged in small talk for a minute, my mind wandered back to the big bastard, Hector Butterfield. I scanned the crowd like I used to. Old habits die hard. Just checking, I told myself. Elvis, commenting that I badly needed a haircut, brought me back to the moment.

Elvis grinned real big and looked at Jerry. Elvis asked him, "So, who were you doing in the Caddy that night?"

Jerry just smiled and said, "A gentleman never tells."

Elvis laughed and we all talked for a while. Dezi was just taking all this in. One moment she was talking to Elvis Presley, and the next minute Mac Davis is introducing her to Cher like she's his oldest friend. Mac is that kind of guy. It was a magical night. I looked around the room at all the famous people relaxed and having a great time. I thought for a minute about the absurdity of it all. Here we were, two dumb-ass high school kids, hanging out with Jerry Lawler, Mac Davis, and Cher, at Graceland helping celebrate Elvis Presley's birthday. You can't make this crap up. I looked at Dezi's smiling eyes as she laughed while listening to a story Cher told about Sonny getting lost in Las Vegas before they were famous. It really doesn't get any better than this. It ended too quickly because, just like Cinderella, Dezi and I had to be home by midnight.

Still, despite all the fun of the evening, I knew that somewhere out there in the darkness that big bastard was hiding, waiting patiently for his chance.

Frog Season

As you might imagine, I started seeing that big bastard almost everywhere I went. Any time I was in a crowd, I would scan it just to make sure he wasn't there. I never saw him when I did my scan. I thought I saw his face on a someone walking down the street as we drove by or I would catch just a glance of someone who moved like him at the far end of the mall. Sometimes, I would think I saw him in the crowd on a news clip on TV. I always saw him when I wasn't looking for him. In retrospect, I do think it was a little much.

Dezi was getting pretty tired of me seeing the big bastard everywhere. I was glad I lived out in the country. With all the critters that lived around my trailer, no one could sneak up on me out there. Some critters would go quiet when someone came, and others would raise a ruckus. There was no sneaking up on me out there. I felt safe, and on the farm, I always carried a gun. In the country, because we had trouble with feral dogs and coyotes, I always carried a pistol when I walked and a rifle when I rode. If the big bastard did show up, I had the means to defend myself. I want to see that big S.O.B. walk off a .45 caliber sucking chest wound.

One of the best things about springtime comes right before they flood the rice fields. Down in rice country, the land is criss-crossed with irrigation ditches and dotted with ponds. Along the banks of those ditches and ponds, in among the snakes and other critters, live the biggest, the meatiest, the tastiest, and the most outspoken, bull frogs on earth. They don't croak at dusk. They roar in the night.

Frog gigging can be done a number of ways. It's one of the few activities where you can use a boat, you can wade, or you can use a pickup truck with equal success. You need, of course, a good-sized cooler filled with an abundance of beer and ice. A beer cooler is always necessary for frog gigging because not only does it hold your beer, it is where you put the frogs you get. Since frog gigging is done only at night, so you will need a really good spotlight with a fresh battery. The way it works is you shine the light along the bank of the ditch or pond to find the frogs. Their eyes reflect light very well, but so do the eyes of a snake. A snake's eyes are a little closer together than those of a frog. It won't take long to learn how to tell the difference. As a rule, you will learn to tell the difference once you have to remove a live water moccasin from the gig. After that, telling the difference between the eyes of a frog and the eyes of a snake isn't really much a problem.

You can use a frog gig which is a twelve-foot-long pole with a barbed trident at the end. Using a gig, once you see the frog's eyes, you creep close and then jab the frog with the gig. The barbs on the trident prevent the frog from slipping off the gig. As a different approach, you can use a .22 rifle. With the rifle, once you see the frog, you shoot the frog. You walk over and pick up the frog. During frog season, using the frog gig is legal. Using the .22 isn't. Both ways are fun.

I took a girlfriend frog gigging once. We were using a .22 from the truck that night. We were doing pretty good, and she enjoyed shooting the frogs. She was a surprisingly good shot. After she shot a frog, I would wade across the ditch and retrieve the frog. Some ditches were thigh deep, and others were only calf deep.

We were having a really good time. She would shoot a frog and I wade through the ditch to go get it. This was working very well, and we were really having a lot of fun. Finally, she shot a frog, and as I waded across the calf-deep ditch, I stepped right smack dab on top of a snake. I couldn't see the snake because of the darkness, but I could feel him wiggling under my foot. I must have stepped on him near his head because I didn't get bit right away. My date, Lisa, called down to me, asking what was wrong. I thought for a minute. If I said snake, she might start shooting in the water to kill the snake. I really didn't want her shooting at the snake I was standing on.

I was in a jam. I have a very well-developed fear of snakes, and I could feel one fighting to get free of my foot. In the car, I had a girl with a rifle just itching to shoot a snake. Finally, knowing I had to do something, I reached down into the muddy water. I grabbed the long, wiggling end of the snake. I yanked as hard as I could and the rest of the snake came free of my foot and in a single motion, I tossed the snake away. He flashed through the light from the spotlight.

"What was that?" Lisa called from the truck.

"Snake," I said in the bravest voice I could muster.

To this very day she thinks I'm not scared of snakes.

As you can see, frog gigging can be a lot of fun. It can be a mind-clearing activity. It's just what I needed to chase that big bastard out of my brain. All thoughts of the big bastard ceased with first sniff of swamp gas and the first mosquito bite.

JD and I have developed frog gigging into a high art. As with duck hunting, we were more than proficient. We had mastered the fine details of a well-executed frog hunt. We were downright professional and usually it wasn't too far into the springtime when we began frog gigging. We had a lot of friends who enjoyed frog gigging, too. Seems folks really enjoy riding around in the back of a pickup truck singing country music, being eaten alive by flocks of mosquitoes, drinking cheap, cold beer, and shooting frogs with an .22 rifle. It ain't legal, but it is good clean fun.

Well, one night JD and I decided to take my old buddy, Jim Ed, out frog gigging with us. I had known Jim Ed for a year or so. We met when I was first getting into CB radios. Dad wanted me to get a tower up at the farm so we could talk on the radio a little easier. Jim Ed put towers up as a kind of sideline business. He actually was a rice farmer, but for some odd reason, he enjoyed climbing towers. I had gone to Mel Redd's slaughterhouse to talk to Jim Ed about putting a hundred-foot tower up at the farm. Jim Ed was at Mel's to hang a new antenna off Mel's tower. Mel's tower was an old hundred-foot tower with old guy wires. Jim Ed went up that tower about as fast as a squirrel runs across a power line. He was at the top in no time and pulling the new antenna up to him when I heard a "twang."

"Did you hear that, Mel?" I said. "Wonder what that was?" I added.

Mel said, "Uh-oh."

Jim Ed must have heard it too because he froze. He didn't move a muscle.

Then, there was another twang. It sounded like a guitar string breaking.

"There it goes again, Mel! What was that?" I said.

From a hundred feet in the air, very clearly I heard Jim Ed quietly and calmly say, "Oh Shit." He began climbing down the tower.

I didn't know what had happened when I heard it, but then I saw that the tower start laying over to one side I figured out what Jim Ed already knew. Two guy wires had broken and now the tower was falling over. Jim Ed, feeling the movement of the tower laying over, was starting to come down the tower really fast.

The whole time the tower laid over, all you could hear was Jim Ed quietly and calmly saying, "Shit. Shit. Shit. Shit."

It all happened really fast. Jim Ed was coming down the tower, and the tower was laying over like a tall tree falls. I felt like I ought to yell "Timber" or something. Jim Ed had really just begun his descent and was only ten feet from the top of the tower when the tower finished its fall. It laid over on the roof of Mel's barn. Watching the tower lay over, it didn't look like it was going very fast, but it was. When Jim Ed landed on the roof of the barn, it made a hell of a racket, and he went clean through the roof. It wasn't a very good barn.

Thankfully, he landed on hay that was stored in the barn. He broke a lot of bones when he went through the roof. It was tough to get to him on account of the hay bales and the collapsed roof. We tried to keep him calm until the EMTs arrived. He was a real trooper. I knew then that we were going to be good friends. Anyone who will drink a beer and have a smoke with you while you are waiting for the EMTs to arrive to take him to the hospital, after a fall like this, is my kind of guy.

The EMS finally showed up. They had a hell of a time getting him out of the barn. They had to move a lot of hay and roof wreckage just to get to him. They called the fire company for help doing that. Mel and I had a couple of beers while they worked cause we knew we'd have to restack the hay when they left. Eventually, they got Jim Ed out of the hay and took him to the hospital. He won't climb towers anymore, and that's why we don't have a tower at the farm. A lot of folks laugh when I tell that story about Jim Ed riding that antenna tower down, but I don't. I don't climb towers either.

Anyway, he's all healed up now except for a little bit of a limp and questionable judgment. We invited him to go frog gigging with us because he's always a lot of fun. JD and I had already hit the ditches pretty hard for the last few weeks, so we needed to let them rest. We decided to go get some frogs off a pond. Gigging in a pond is a little tougher than gigging out of a truck, but it's still lots of fun. Jim Ed hadn't gigged out of a boat, so this would be fun.

There was a pond down at Otwell that was kind of secluded. It was possible that JD and I were the only folks who knew about it. It was another one of those places that if you didn't know it was there, you'd never find it. It was deep in rice country. That meant it would be thick with snakes, but ought to have some good frogs on it.

It was about nine in the evening by the time we got to the pond and put the boat in the water. That's about the right time to start gigging. You have to wait till the mosquitoes get really active, and that means it has to be good and dark. It took just a few more minutes to load the lawn chair, the cooler, three or four gigs, extra beer, and the lights with extra batteries into the boat. JD carefully put the trolling motor on the stern of the boat, and I made sure we had paddles. The battery of the trolling motor had been known to run out of juice on the far side of the pond. Paddles can come in real handy. We used the trolling motor to creep around the pond without making too much noise. Frogs will dive if they hear you coming.

JD was running the motor, and I ran the light. Jim Ed was gigging frogs. You could tell that no one had gigged this pond so far this year because all of the frogs were huge. Most were twelve inches or more, from nose-to-toes. We were getting a frog every few minutes. When you shined the light around the edge of the pond, hundreds of eyes, frogs, snakes, and unknowns, shined back at us. This was going to be a great frog hunt.

Everyone was having a great time, and we were going through the beer at a pretty rapid clip. Even though he was a farm boy, Jim Ed was little squeamish about getting frogs off the frog gig, but he came around after a couple of beers. It took him a little longer to realize some things. One thing was that, if you are drinking a beer from a cooler full of dead frogs, you need to check the top of your beer can for frog guts before you start drinking it. Jim Ed squealed like a girl and barfed just a little when he discovered frog guts on the top of his beer can. JD and I got a good laugh out of that. Generally speaking, folks won't make that mistake twice.

I was running the spotlight and lit up a snake. Usually when I lit up a snake, I just kept going. On this one JD and I both immediately knew it was a snake, but Jim Ed didn't. I paused on it. I didn't say anything, but I looked at JD. I could see what he was thinking so I wasn't surprised when he grabbed one of the extra gigs and steered the boat so he had the best angle on the snake. Striking with the quickness of a cobra, JD gigged the snake. It looked like there was an explosion in the water as the battle began. This was a huge water moccasin and it fought desperately to escape. That snake didn't get this big by being a pushover. JD had gigged him behind the head, so the tail was thrashing madly about trying to escape. JD strained to lift the snake out of the water. This was a monster snake. I shined the light on it so that Jim Ed could see it real well. JD, being an ass, swung this slithering, wiggling beast in real close to Jim Eds face so he could get a real up-close look at it.

While JD, laughing like hell, was holding the six-foot-long, writhing, monster water moccasin right in front of Jim Ed, the snake finally managed to fight its way free of the gig. Apparently, it wasn't gigged quite as securely as we thought it was. It dropped straight down into the boat. It very nearly landed in Jim Ed's lap. When the snake fell free from the gig, JD lost his balance and almost fell overboard. Jim Ed used his cat like reflexes to promptly jump out of the boat. Dropping my light, I was hopping all over my end of the little boat to avoid the snake when suddenly I felt a searing pain in my foot.

"He got me," I hollered to JD.

JD, having recovered his balance, immediately stood up again and drew his .357 pistol. He began blasting away with his gun, blowing holes in the bottom of my boat as he attempted to shoot the fast-moving snake. It's a lot harder to hit a moving snake with a pistol than you would think. Jim Ed, swimming like a man possessed, was halfway across the pond heading for the landing. JD paused to reload as water began to fill the boat through the holes he had shot in the bottom. I got ahold of one of the boat paddles, and managed to fling a very pissed off water moccasin overboard. He disappeared into the black water.

"Where'd he get you?" JD asked urgently as he holstered his gun and pointed the boat toward the landing.

"The foot. Man, this hurts! He must have got me good. It feels like he's still got me," I said, feeling supremely sick. I had always heard the snake venom hurt a lot. I wondered if death by water moccasin was a dramatic head spinning, spitting and vomiting, convulsing death or a death where you just sort of drift off. Whatever it was, I hoped it would be quick. This snake bite really, really hurt.

I searched for the spotlight that I had dropped while dodging the snake. Finally, I found it. I got a hold of the spotlight and quickly turned it on. I shined the light down on my foot and, in addition to a staggering amount of blood, saw the gig with the twelve-foot pole still attached, sticking out of the side of my foot. I was greatly relieved to find that I had not been snake bit at all. With the prospect of my imminent demise lifted my relief was short lived because the pain was rapidly becoming much worse.

Apparently, while I was jumping around trying to avoid getting snake bit, I had managed to gig my own foot with one of the frog gigs that was laying in the bottom of the boat. The gig was sunk about as deeply as it could go into the side of my foot. Trying to sound calm, I asked JD to please get us to the landing before the boat sank completely. I had doubts about my ability to swim with a frog gig stuck in my foot. In seconds, JD was running the trolling motor flat out to get us back to the landing. That, I should add, is not very fast. While it is obvious why trolling motors are known for their stealth, it is equally clear why they are not generally known for their speed.

By the time we got to the landing, our speed was greatly diminished, and the boat was about two-thirds full of water. JD and Jim Ed helped me out of the boat and into the back of the truck. We were all soaking wet; Jim Ed from his swim, and JD and me from riding in the sinking boat. Moving was very painful because as we moved, so did the gig with the twelve-foot pole.

Once we made it to the bed of the truck, JD looked closely at it. With an optimistic tone in his voice and as he reached for the pole, he said, "I think I can get it out."

Before he could finish the sentence, I had my gun pressed to his forehead. "You pull it out and I'll blow your brains across the pond," I said with true and deep malice in my heart.

Jim Ed, looking at all the blood, said, "We got to get him to Doc Wagner's before he bleeds out! He only lives about five miles away!"

Until now, bleeding out had not entered my mind, but there was a lot of blood. I didn't know Dr. Wagner. I had never heard of him, but I figured he must be a local doctor practicing at Harrisburg or Wiener. Anyway, he could probably get the bleeding stopped. The gig hurt so much that I was pretty happy that we didn't have to drive all the way back to Jonbur to get this thing out. Five miles beat twenty-five miles any day!

JD and Jim Ed pulled the screws out that attached the gig to the pole. That was painful because both JD and Jim Ed, being somewhat panicked, were yanking the gig around a lot while they worked to remove the screws. More than once, one of them slipped and jabbed my foot pretty hard with the screwdriver. I hollered both times about it. JD said to quit bitching. The screwdriver wounds weren't bleeding near as much as the frog gig wound, he said. Once the pole was off the gig, it was a lot easier to bandage up my foot even though because of the gig we couldn't take the shoe off. We left the boat at the pond and I rode in the bed of the truck. We figured that it would be a pretty good idea to keep my foot elevated. The bleeding seemed to be under control at this point. Jim Ed rode with me to help me keep my foot propped up on the tailgate of the truck.

That night, I learned a lesson about having JD drive after he's been drinking. It's not a good idea. We were in my truck that night, and now JD was driving my truck like my life depended on it. Jim Ed and I were in the back getting bounced all over the place and choking on the dust. I had my flasks, so I was sharing my flask with Jim Ed some. The whisky was taking the edge of off the pain a little and helping to keep Jim Ed calm while JD drove. Finally, we hit pavement and JD slammed on the brakes. Jim Ed and I, sitting near the tailgate, were both thrown violently against the back of the cab of the truck when it stopped. JD jumped out and announced that he didn't know where Doc Wagner lives. JD and Jim Ed switched places.

I learned another lesson. Having Jim Ed drive after he's been drinking isn't a good idea either. Jim Ed was an old soul, rice farmer kind of guy. Rather than seeing a pickup truck as a means of personal transport that should be driven with care and is expected to last some number of years, he saw a pickup truck as an expendable thing that gets replaced every year because it gets beat all to hell. There is a good reason that no one buys a used pickup truck from a rice farmer. Like JD, Jim Ed was driving as if my life were in the balance. He flew down the highway at an unconscionable rate of speed. JD and I shared my flask. I worked on getting religion because the way Jim Ed was driving, I thought I might need it soon. I was drinking the whisky pretty aggressively because I needed the relief from the pain of the frog gig. Each bump we hit caused the gig to move a little, and that was unbelievably painful. I shared the flask with JD because it was the neighborly thing to do and I hoped it would keep JD calm. Jim Ed's driving was a bit erratic.

We were roaring down Harrisburg highway when, with no warning, Jim Ed locked up the rear wheels and began his turn onto another road just a fuzz early. We spun out and went through a shallow ditch, took out a yield sign and bunch of mailboxes. JD and I were thrown and bounced about as if we were just another empty beer can in the bed of the truck. When we emerged from the other side, everything in the bed of the truck, beer cans, gas cans, tire tools and us, was momentarily airborne. The landing was very painful. Once we stopped moving, Jim Ed dropped the truck into first gear and squealed the tires as we took off down the street. JD and I began to drink the bourbon more rapidly. At this point, both of us had, more-or-less, found religion. We repented our all sins. Finally, we arrived at Doc Wagner's house. We skidded to a stop in front of his house. Jim Ed leaped out of the truck. and took off running up to the door. JD and I follow, slower because we're sort of drunk, and I only had one good foot.

Mrs. Wagner, in her robe, came to the door moments later. She had obviously been sleeping. She greeted Jim Ed and admonished him for banging on the door so late at night. Jim Ed explained that there had been a horrible accident and we need Doc right away. Doc, she said, was out with Eugene and Morris. She wasn't sure exactly where they might be. "Perhaps," she suggested, "you could look at the Number One Club. They like to go there."

All three of us returned to the truck. JD, having had enough of Jim Ed's driving, said, "Aaarrrg! I'm driving now, matey!" For some unknown reason, JD was talking like a pirate now. This night was getting weird. This was not a good sign.

Jim Ed returned to the bed of the truck with me. JD fired up the truck. We cut a donut and headed back to the highway. My foot was really, really hurting now. It was throbbing like no one's business and blood, from both the frog gig and the screwdriver wounds, was showing through the bandages. We had managed to stick the cooler in the back of the truck with us before we abandoned the boat back at the pond. The flasks were now empty; we were out of whisky. Jim Ed and I both got a beer out of the cooler. It occurred to Jim Ed that ice might help my foot, so we dangled my foot in the cooler with ice, the beer, and fourteen dead frogs all of which were at least twelve inches, nose-to-toes.

The Number One Club was only about thirty minutes away. It's just off Highway One about a half-mile down a gravel road. JD, or rather my truck, suffered an unfortunate encounter with an oak tree as we turned into the Club's parking lot. JD misjudged the turn just a bit. While executing a solid power slide into the parking lot, he successfully removed the mirror from my driver's side door and dented the door and part of the bed very nicely. I have to give credit where credit is due, he managed to stop before actually running into the building. Again, we all three got out and went in the club. Walking with the gig in my foot was becoming more and more painful. It was throbbing like hell. There was a band playing inside, so now it was throbbing to the beat of the music. To actually get in the club to look for Doc Wagner, we each had to pay the two-dollar cover charge. My wallet was in the car, so Jim Ed fronted me a couple of bucks. The guy at the door asked me to try not to bleed on the floor too much.

Inside, I got a table and elevated my foot on it, while JD and Jim Ed roamed the loud, dark room looking for Doc Wagner. I was feeling a little lightheaded. It must be from blood loss, I thought. A waitress came by and I ordered us a round of beer while they searched. I found it interesting that when you are already drunk, you rarely get carded. A couple of folks wanted to know how I got a frog gig in my foot. One guy actually asked me if it hurt much. Another one or two commented that my foot looked like it really hurt, and I assured them that they were right. It did really hurt. One couple insisted that I do a couple of tequila shots with them, you know, for the pain. They were nice. Finally, JD and Jim Ed came back. No Doc Wagner in the joint. JD paid our tab, we shot gunned our beer and we headed out again.

Jim Ed said, "I've only got one more place he might be. If he's not there, we're screwed. We'll have to go to Jonbur."

Both JD and Jim Ed tried to get in the cab of the truck. Both complained about the other's driving. Finally, they settled it with rock-paper-scissors. Jim Ed was driving. JD climbed in the back. We put my foot back in the cooler with the ice, beer, and frogs. We roared down the highway, and all the way back through Harrisburg. Jim Ed, again cutting curve just a little too close, got a school bus shelter and some more mailboxes. We skidded to a halt in the gravel parking lot at the Harrisburg Veterinary Clinic. The lights were on in the building.

Jim Ed, seeing the old, beat-up pickup that he knew to be Doc Wagner's, hollered out the door, "Pay Dirt! He's here!"

For a third time, we clambered out of the truck. JD helped me. My foot was really throbbing now. Jim Ed banged on the door. Doc Wagner came to the door in just a moment. He recognized Jim Ed and greeting him. Doc let us into the building, and asked why we were in such a tizzy.

Jim Ed referenced the frog gig in my foot. I held my foot up so he could get a good look at it. He motioned me into an exam room and carefully removed some of the bandage. He commented on how deeply it was stuck in. He looked at me and said, "Son, I think you need to see a doctor."

"Aren't you a doctor?" I said to Doc Walker.

Annoyed, Doc Wagner looked coldly at Jim Ed.

"Jim Ed, I keep telling you. I'm a veterinarian. There's a difference. This man needs a medical doctor, probably a surgeon," he countered.

At this point, it is about two hours since I gigged my foot. I have bled all over Harrisburg, Arkansas. The foot is throbbing and I can't walk. We have run back and forth through Harrisburg, Arkansas, looking for a man, who we thought was a medical doctor, only to find that he is a veterinarian. Turns out, the nearest medical doctor is at a hospital in Jonbur, twenty-five minutes away. I looked at Jim Ed with utter amazement.

Jim Ed saw the look I was giving him. "He cured Ed Healy's dose of the clap. I thought he could get a frog gig out of your stupid foot without any problem."

"Jim Ed," Doc Wagner said, "I thought we agreed that we wouldn't share that with anyone else." Turning to me, Doc said, "Ed is my nephew. Got a little dose up in Missouri a few months ago."

JD was just shaking his head.

Twenty minutes later, what was left of my truck is sitting in the parking lot at the ER in Jonbur. By now, it is one in the morning. We are waiting for the on-call radiologist to come in to consult with the surgeon who has come in and is about to perform surgery to remove the frog gig from my foot. I was praying that Dad's partner, Dr. Green would be on call.

I heard the door to the exam room open behind me. I heard the sound of a long and weary exhale.

A very familiar voice, speaking slowly and sounding for all the world like he was announcing the fall of Rome, said, "You're going to need to stay at the house while this heals."

I felt horrible. Dad had not even seen my truck yet and didn't know about the bullet holes in the bottom of the boat we left abandoned at the pond.

This was going to get worse. Everyone, including me, had already forgotten about the cooler of dead frogs in the back of my truck. After a couple of days in the hot sun, whoever opened that cooler was in for a real bad experience.

Damn.

Storm Runoff

My foot had me laid up for about two weeks. I lived at Mom and Dad's house and slept on the couch in the basement. Mom had turned my room into a library when I went to live at the farm. I couldn't drive so Dezi came by every morning to take me to school and dropped me off in the afternoon. I usually sat on the back porch and did homework or something. Finally, my foot was healed enough for me to get around, so it was back-to-the-farm for me. Mom survived my stay at the house without any side effects. Dad told me he was proud of me. I was happy. Mom seemed genuinely sad for me to go, but the cattle needed tending to, and I was pretty sure that though he would gladly collect his pay for tending them for a couple of weeks, Enid never actually did anything to take care of them while I was laid up.

The truck was in the shop again and the gravel roads out at the farm was no place for a pink Caddy so Dad dropped me at the farm. I made arrangements to catch a ride into town in the mornings for school with the milkman who serviced the grocery. I drove the tractor to the store at four-thirty and got to school at about eight o'clock. I didn't even have time to start making some extra money to repair the truck until school was out.

One Saturday while I was visiting at Mom and Dad's house, JD dropped by. He and some of the other guys were going over to the airport to watch the skydivers. Arkansas State had a skydiving team, and they were practicing at the airport. Watching them practice was a great way to spend an afternoon.

We met Pearson, Bradley, Francis, Becky, and Geno, at VFW club parking lot. This may have been the first time Becky had been back to the airport since she and Bobcat scattered the ashes. We were set up near the airport but not actually on the grounds of the airport. We parked around back of the VFW so we could set up lawn chairs under some shade trees and get the cooler out. Everyone made sure to pour their beer into a cup, and then put the beer can in the trash bag. If no one saw a beer can, no one would call the cops on us.

We were sitting there drinking beer and watching the skydivers prep for their jumps. No one was talking about anything much, just sort of visiting while we watched the skydivers check out their gear. As always with these guys, conversations became an exercise in free association.

222

While everyone was talking about what they thought the biggest differences between an airplane engine and a car engine were, out of nowhere Francis said to the entire group, as if it was a public service announcement, "So, Slim Edwards down at the pool hall says that Mary Higgins is a hermaphrodite." For anyone else, that would be an odd statement, but for Francis, it was the norm.

Becky just stared at him, not knowing how to react. Slim was one of the pool sharks at Francis' father's pool hall. Mary was a super pool player who routinely beat Slim.

"Mary's a what?" JD said.

"Slim says that Mary is a hermaphrodite," Francis repeated in a way intended to imply that he knew what a hermaphrodite was.

The skydivers had finished their prep and were all walking over toward the plane. I was torn between watching the skydivers enter the plane and watching this conversation play out. The twin-engine plane, the skydivers were about to climb into, had a door missing. One of the motors was already running, but the other had not been started yet. Everyone watched, as one-by-one, they got into the plane.

"What in the hell is a hermorpa-what ever?" Bradley asked.

"Hermaphrodite. That's a woman who likes other women," Pearson replied.

"Really?" said Becky, not exactly believing what she was hearing.

"Bullshit!" said Geno. "No, That's not a hermaphrodite. That's a dyke. Slim's just pissy because Mary beats his ass again."

JD, smiling, chimed in. "Does that make him a masochist?"

"What's a masochist?" I asked.

Becky, shaking her head, put her face in her hands realizing that while there may be a limit to genius, there appears to be no limit to stupidity.

All the skydivers were in the plane now. The second engine started with a belch of blue smoke. Bradly and Pearson looked at each other. They knew that blue smoke was not a good thing to see when starting an engine.

"Plane needs a ring job," Bradly commented to no one in particular. Pearson nodded in agreement. The rest of us just watched silently.

"A masochist is someone who likes to get their ass beat," came the reply to my question.

Just then someone on the CB radio said something about the weather. We always had the CB on so we would know what was going on. JD had his CB hooked up to a loudspeaker on his truck. When someone made a comment about the weather, we all heard it over the loudspeaker, but no one recognized the call sign, so no one paid much attention to the comment.

"You know, like Jerry Quarry," Geno said with a grin. Jerry Quarry was a professional boxer who got beat to a bloody pulp in every fight he fought.

"That's cold-blooded," JD said smiling at Geno.

"No, JD, damn it," Francis said. "You guys are confused. Hermaphrodites are girls who dress like boys. Have you ever seen Mary in a dress?"

Becky, who wore jeans nearly every day, was utterly amazed that these people were her friends. I saw that Becky was staring at Francis with unbelieving eyes. I was pretty sure Francis didn't know what he was talking about.

"That would make her a transvestite?" Geno said, looking around for confirmation.

Bradly spoke up. "No, according to Lou Reed, transvestites are guys who dress like girls. You know, like 'Take a Walk on the Wild Side,'" Bradley said, referencing a song that was popular at the time. Bradley was a rather worldly guy, so I thought that he was probably right.

"Maybe Mary is just a transvestite and you just don't know it," JD proposed. Everyone was quiet for a minute while that soaked in. The plane had taxied to the end of the runway.

Pearson finally spoke up. "Slim told you Mary was a hermaphrodite?" he asked Francis.

"Yep, loves other women," Francis replied confidently. Becky was looking off in the distance now, biting her tongue, trying not to laugh.

"JD, you know Mary has a child," Pearson said as he watched the plane throttle up and begin a takeoff roll down the runway.

"Well, that does complicate things," JD smiled.

"If you remember, Francis," Bradley continued, "Slim also told you that girls don't fart and can't get pregnant on the first time."

Becky looked at Bradley. I was having a pretty good time just watching Becky's reaction to the whole conversation. I suspected that Becky knew more about all this than anyone else there. But being pretty smart, she knew that these clowns would not understand things even if she explained it very slowly.

Francis ignored Pearson, and answered Bradley. "Yeah, So what's your point?"

I disengaged from the conversation as I watched the plane, full of skydivers, roar down the runway. I didn't even wonder if any of them were hermaphrodites or transvestites. I didn't give a tinker's damn about that. At about two-thirds the way down the runway, the plane lifted into the air and the landing gear began to retract into the body of the plane. The plane, climbing slowly, turned to the south. Conversation ceased and we all watched the plane fly away until it was just a tiny, black speck in the blue sky.

Everyone sat watching the plane climb into the distant clouds. Someone changed the subject, and several individual conversations broke out. You couldn't hear the plane at all now and all talk was about fishing or frog gigging or cars.

I didn't engage in the conversations at that point. My mind was in the plane. I was stuck on the thought that there were some folks in that plane that were going to jump out of it when it flew over the airport. They were going to jump out, just for the hell of it, jump out. That captivated me. I wondered what was going through their minds when they went out the door. I wondered if they were scared. I wondered what it felt like to be falling through the air. I wondered what it sounded like as the wind rushed past you as you fell. I don't know how long it was, but after a bit, someone said, "Look, there it is." It was a lone black dot, far away in the blue, blue sky.

Sure enough, way, way, way up in the sky, that black dot was a plane. It was the plane with the skydivers. My mind was with them. I could smell the air up there. I had flown up to seventy-five-hundred feet with Bobcat once. The air smells different up there. I imagined that someone was sitting in the door now. They take one of the doors off of a skydiving plane so it's easier to jump out when they are flying. The plane was overhead now. We heard the pilot cut the engines back. We strained our eyes. Nothing, nothing, and then just a moment or two later, even smaller black specks could be seen coming from the plane and falling away. Some spread out, some seemed to be coming together. The engine noise came back up. The plane banked away from the skydivers and flew away.

We watched the tiny specks fall. Five or six appeared to converge for a few seconds. They were falling together in some sort of formation. Then, while they were still high in the sky, they split apart. Each one flew away in a different direction before opening their parachutes. Each parachute, one at a time. Streamed off the skydiver and blossomed in the sky. It reminded me of a bursting firework in a night sky. Parachutes were everywhere. Though we didn't know how many people had actually jumped out of the plane, we counted thirteen parachutes open and could see no more falling specks. What an amazing sight! There was no more talk of hermaphrodites.

Everyone was just chilling and watching the skydivers. It was hot and muggy with big, fluffy white clouds about, but we were under some shade trees behind the VFW. We all watched as the plane landed. Thirty minutes later, as the skydivers began prepping for their second jump, a voice came over the CB radio looking for "Hunter." It was "Hound Dog." Hunter was JD's handle on the radio. JD got up and went to his truck. He answered the call saying, "You got Hunter, back at you."

That was CB talk for "This is JD, what's up?"

"There's big storms over Dallas. It's going to be a busy night," Hound dog said through the static.

"A four Roger D, Out," JD replied. That was CB talk for "I understand, Good-bye." Seems to me it would have been just as easy to say "Gotcha," but on the CB everyone talked in a code of sorts.

On hearing that message, we all started to move. We were, after all, storm spotters. We would be working that night. We weren't in a hurry, but everyone did have to go and prep for the night. There was plenty of time, but now was the time to start moving. Storms worth mentioning over Dallas meant that we'd have bad storms to watch tonight. Everyone would soon be headed to headquarters to get a briefing on the details of the weather and to get ready for a long, perhaps dangerous night.

Civil Defense Headquarters served as our Storm Center. On the radio, Storm Center went by "Center." About thirty of our members gathered at four-thirty in the afternoon. Mr. Grimmet gave us the low down on the weather and how it was likely to develop. An area of very low pressure was running rapidly up the frontal boundary that divided our hot, humid air from the cool, dry air pushing down from Colorado and Kansas. A line of thunderstorms was forming along that line, and as the low-pressure center pushed up the line, storms were expected to be severe. The front was projected to pass through Jonbur at about ten o'clock. We could expect storms to start at eight or so. Temperatures would remain high until the front passed, then high pressure and cool dry air would be in place and the storm threat would be over. We would be advised and directed by operators at the radar station. Everyone checked their gear, and at six-thirty, we deployed to our posts.

JD and I were ready. We were in his truck and parked in our appointed location by seven o'clock. Already lightning was visible in the distance. In the truck with us we had our standard gear. Both of us had a lensatic compass. We always used mine because it was easier to use. We had a thermometer for temperature readings. We had water and some snacks. We had several radios. One was our standard civil defense band radio. The other was a police scanner that we used to monitor other weather-related operations. Under the dash, JD had his CB radio mounted. There was a giant whip antenna outside mounted on the truck's toolbox. I always kind of thought that thing was as much a lightning rod as an antenna. In the dashboard was a Craig AM/FM eight-track stereo. It was one of the best car stereos that White Dog Record Shop sold. I helped JD install it. It worked really well with the custom speakers he put in, too. On nights like this, we didn't listen to any eight tracks. We had the civil defense radio going as well as the scanner. We tuned the FM radio to KFIN so we could get weather updates there. Usually, we got more frequent weather information from KFIN than we got from the "official" sources. KFIN got good radar reports out of the weather service in Memphis.

It started getting dark at seven-thirty or so. To the southwest, out in the distance, we could see more and more lightning as the storms approached. The crazy thing about these storms is that they come in cells. Cells are big, localized storms with lightning, high winds, and very, very heavy rain. These things give birth to tornadoes. Usually, when one of these fronts came through, we would have three or four cells that come near the city. We had to watch them closely. Usually, only one of the cells would actually come through town. Sometimes there would be more, but usually it was just the one.

When your position is in a cell, you can't make any observations at all. It is just time to hunker down. If there is a funnel cloud that forms in one that you are currently in, there is only one way to find out there is a funnel cloud on you. You find out it's a funnel cloud when it blows you away. This is because the only other way to find out is by hearing it on the radio. When you are in a cell, the static drowns everything out on the radio. You won't be able to get the message. Everything is over when the temperature drops about thirty degrees in about five minutes. At sixty degrees, you aren't ever going to see much of a funnel cloud.

Having lived through a tornado just a couple of years ago, most of us were always a little on edge watching the storms progress across rice country toward Jonbur. The lightning in the storms made it possible to see how huge the storms were in terms of size, and the amount of lightning in the storms gave a pretty good indication as to how bad the storms were going to be. You could get a sense of the depth and height of the cell when lightning flashed inside of it. It always looked like some sort of flashing Godzilla monster to me. When I saw the really tall storms, I always felt tiny. As we looked to the southwest on this particular night, JD and I both realized pretty early on that this was going to be a bad night. The monster we could see flashing in the distance was as tall as I have ever seen. It wasn't raining yet and the wind hadn't come up either, but at the very same instant, JD and I both looked nervously around our position as if to find a more sheltered spot. We knew we couldn't take a sheltered spot. We had to stay in the open so we could see the horizon when called upon.

When one of these storms comes in, the first thing that happens is that lightning creeps closer to you. It always seems like it's five miles away one second, and right on top of you the next. There is nothing gradual to its arrival at your location. It is a sudden thing. Some of the lightning is cloud-to-cloud, but the really scary stuff is cloud-to-ground. That's what will turn you into a pile of ashes. The whip antenna on the truck always looked like a lightning rod to me, and I know that they say that the rubber tires and metal skin of the truck protect you, but a little voice in me keeps saying that lightning will fry your ass.

Until the rain starts, we always have the windows open. It's cooler that way. In storm spotting training, one of the things we learned was that in the last second or two before lightning strikes a position, there will be the distinct smell of sulfur in the air. With the windows open, as the storm approached, I was constantly sniffing for sulfur. I don't know why I did that. It's not like I could jump out of the truck and get on the ground, or perhaps roll up the window before lightning hit me. Watching a cell with heavy lightning come in always gave me a lot of nervous energy. I needed to move, but we had to stay in the truck.

Next, the wind shifts as the storm takes control of the area. This isn't the shift that cools the air. No, this is a humid wind and it offers little in relief from the heat. It's like sitting in a steam room with a hair dryer blowing in your face. Sometimes, it blows some dust. If the storm happens to be in daylight and you are overlooking dry fields, you may see a little of a dust storm coming across the fields. We usually report that on the radio. If it's nighttime, the mosquitoes will be blown out by this wind. Mosquitoes don't do well in wind. There will be wind gusts so strong that they rock the truck, and blow so much road sand that you have to roll up the windows. I know it's stupid, but I always feel a little safer from the lightning once we have rolled up the windows. The wind may be the only effect of the storm that you can actually feel for five minutes or thirty-five minutes. The time varies. The thing that happens last is the rain.

There is something amazing about watching a hard rain advance across an open plain. Rice country is pretty much an open plain. It is some of the flattest land in the country, and watching a wall of water come across it is incredible. Even if it is ten at night, in the light of the lightning you can watch the wall of rain approach. Rain beneath a storm looks like a gray, lace curtain suspended from the clouds. As it advances across farms, you can watch as houses and barns fade away as the gray curtain advances on your position. The wind gives the wall of rain the look of a frayed-and-tattered lace curtain blowing in the wind. As it gets close to you, first you get a few raindrops falling at random intervals. Sometimes these are tiny raindrops, and other times they seem to be the size of grapefruit. Sometimes they are so large they make a very solid sound as they hit the top of the truck. This may go on for a few minutes. Eventually, it will very suddenly become a downpour of biblical proportions. You will not be able to see out of the truck at all. With the lightning exploding trees near you, and the wind rocking the truck like a tiny ship on a boiling sea, this time can be very unnerving. The cell is right on top of you. That's not a good thing. The first time it happens always shake a person up. After that, all the fun and excitement is gone out of storm spotting. Now, it's real, too real for some. We still do it, though. We do it because it's an important job during a storm.

On this night, JD and I watched the light show presented during the approach of the storm. "It is bad," I thought. "But, I've seen worse." Whether or not it was true, that's what we always told ourselves when watching a storm come in. "It's not that bad," I'd lie to myself. Tonight, it was that bad. It was really bad, but it looked like the worst of the storm would miss Jonbur.

The wind with the storm came up, and it wasn't awful. It appeared that the body of the storm was a bit to the west of us. Jonbur was getting a hell of a soaking, but it looked like the worst violence of the storm would miss the town. Perhaps the worst thing about this storm would be runoff and flash flooding.

At about ten-twenty-five, Storm Center called to us on the radio. JD answered with "Sixteen, Copy." We were Team Sixteen and Copy meant that we had heard them. Lightning played hell with the radios. Static from lightning near and far made understanding each other more than a little difficult. That's why code was used. The less talk, the better.

Storm Center called again. "Sixteen, Sight 270, One point five Mikes, Over."

Decoded, that meant that Center wanted us to look out on a heading of 270 degrees off of magnetic north and report what we saw in that direction about a mile-and-a-half out.

I got my lensatic compass out. JD and I looked out of the truck windshield on the heading of 270 degrees. When Storm Center wanted a sighting, that generally meant that they had a hook echo on the radar at the location described. They were looking for a visual confirmation, looking for information as to the funnel cloud's direction of travel, and whether or not it was on the ground before they issued a warning or began moving resources.

JD and I both looked closely at the night sky. The rain wasn't on us yet, so we had very good vision in the light of the lightning. We carefully searched the night sky for a funnel cloud silhouetted against the dark storm clouds, but none could be found. Funnel clouds that have not reached the ground are generally easier to spot at night because the shattered rain in the funnel makes it appear white in the night. Against the dark clouds and illuminated by the lightning, they aren't hard to find. A funnel cloud on the ground is always black due to the dirt and crap it picks up. They are harder to see against the dark clouds. Sometimes you find them because you see the power lines sparking like mad as they get blown down. Funnel clouds can be big and fat, or just tiny daggers barely reaching the ground. I have seen them a quarter mile across at the bottom, and I have seen them a couple hundred feet across at the bottom. Each one is different. Finally, after looking for several minutes, we reported that we found nothing. Storm Center acknowledged.

We watched the storm continue along its course and listened as Storm Center asked other spotters for sightings on various headings. There seem to have been a number of hook echos in this storm, but none threatened Jonbur proper. The police scanner told us what parts of town had lost power, and where trees were down. We were glad there were no reports of damage you expect from funnel clouds. Where we were, we barely got rain. Inside Jonbur, they got tons of rain. Storm runoff was causing flash floods all over town. The ditches would be raging torrents of water.

With the storm had mostly passed us, we relaxed some. It was still giving it hell to the north and west of us. We heard on the police scanner that someone had taken advantage of the storm to break into a drugstore out in Nettleton. During bad thunderstorms and heavy snow falls, crooks like to rob drugstores because of all the disruption that is already going on. Apparently, the alarm at this drugstore still functioned and a cop had showed up in time to see the burglar drive away at a high rate of speed. Now the cops were in pursuit of the car with the burglar. We had prepped for the storm by bringing a cooler. Since the storm was over, we got a couple of bottles of water and some corn chips to munch on while we listened to the chase. The burglar was in a blue Dodge Dart. Dodge is a Chrysler product. Dodge cars run like scalded dogs, but the cop was in Dodge too, so he kept up just fine. Just a couple of minutes after the cop transmitted the tag number. It wasn't too long before police headquarters reported back that the car had been reported stolen yesterday in Paragould. The burglar was giving it hell all over town. He was on his way out of town down Wood Street when he turned onto Woodsprings Road. He hit a flooded patch and hydroplaned. He wrapped that Dodge Dart around a tree. We heard the report come over the radio.

"I'll bet that's near Betsy's house!" JD said excitedly.

The cop chasing him reported that the guy climbed out of the car and took off down toward the creek. He was going to give chase. Then, there was silence because the cop was out of his car.

JD and I stayed on our post drinking our water and critiquing the guy's route and driving skills as we understood them from the radio reports from the cops. We speculated on what we would do to escape if someone was chasing us over there. We were waiting to hear reports as other cops got into the search.

"I would have stayed on Wood Street and taken it to the bypass, and then down into rice country," I said.

JD agreed that made more sense. "Yep, get them in the mud," he said. But then on second thought he added, "A car won't go far in that mud, but you know what? The burglar was in a car too. He wasn't in a truck."

Just then a voice came on the scanner. It was a civilian reporting that the office and the robber had fought at the creek and both had fallen in the creek and were being swept downstream.

I looked at JD and he looked at me. Because we gigged along all the creeks and ditches around town, we both knew that the creek dumped into Big Ditch. A ton of other ditches dumped into Big Ditch down just off the ridge, too. The water would be moving really fast, and if you weren't a really good swimmer, you'd drown in no time. It was a tall and clean-cut bank pretty much from there to the Saint Francis River with nothing to grab hold of to get out. JD and

I were probably the only folks in town who knew exactly where the burglar and the cop were going to come out and how to get there.

I grabbed the civil defense radio and tried to raise Storm Center. The static was still pretty bad, and we didn't really have code words or shorthand to communicate what we needed to tell them. We were trying to tell them that the cop and the burglar were going to get dumped out into Big Creek down Culberhouse Road, but the static was too bad. They thought we were reporting something about the storm out that way, and so they were responding by moving spotters into position to observe that area.

We could hear the police on the scanner moving officers to try to get the guys out of the creek. The creek was a fast moving torrent of water. The police didn't know where it went and were madly trying to locate the two men being carried away. We could hear the confusion on the radio, and worst yet, because we knew where the creek went, we knew the police and fire department were looking for them in the wrong places.

JD fired the truck up and said, "We gotta go help those guys."

We took off to a spot on the creek we knew that was before the place where it dumped into the Big Ditch. It was a sure thing the cops weren't going to get to those guys, so we had to do it. We brainstormed how to do it on the way. The big problem was how to get a hold of them as they swept by.

It was less than five minutes before we were at the spot where we thought they would get swept by. I jumped out and dug around in the toolbox in the bed of the truck. I found a tow strap in the toolbox. JD fished around behind the seat of the truck and found the light we used for frog gigging. JD shined the frog light up the creek so that maybe we could see the guys as they came down the channel. The water was going past us like a runaway freight train. I looked at it and knew that there was little chance a person could survive in it long enough to get to where we were. If the burglar or the cop did come by, they would likely be already drowned. If they had drowned, they would be underwater, and we would be combing the Saint Francis River bottom tomorrow looking for their body. That we could only save one was a thought that floated in the back of my head. I didn't want to acknowledge it at all, but I was pretty sure at least one man was going to drown tonight.

As all that was going through my mind, JD called out, "Got him!"

I looked up and sure enough, JD had someone in his spotlight splashing down the creek. From the way he moved, you could tell he was exhausted. As he fought to stay above water, he saw us on the bank and tried to maneuver closer to our side. He made some progress toward us, and I got ready. I was going to toss him the tow strap as he went by. I could tell I wasn't going to be close enough for a sure shot. I inched just a little into the water because this would be his only chance. Still, it wasn't enough. I crept just a fuzz closer. The water was bringing him to me much faster than I realized. The water was tearing at my legs trying to pull me downstream when he was blasting past me. I threw the tow strap to him. He made one desperate grab and got it with one hand. The current pulled him past and I braced to pull him in. I leaned way back and dug my heels into the soft mud because I anticipated a big pull.

I didn't anticipate big enough. It wasn't a big pull at all. It was a king-hell yank. If we had tied the tow strap to the truck, I think this guy would have pulled the truck in. I'm not really sure how it happened, but now I was in the ditch connected to him by the tow strap and barreling down the churning water toward Big Ditch. This was not what I had expected. When he went past me, rather than me pulling him out, he had pulled me in.

Well, damn.

I could tell he was beat, exhausted, done. I pulled myself toward him using the tow strap as the churning water hurled us downstream. Finally, I got a hold of him by the hair of the head. He was starting to go limp. I worked to get him on his back while I kicked my shoes off and ditched my gun. I got us pointed downstream and did the sidestroke at an angle toward the bank. I had him by the hair and dragged him behind me. It was a long, hard, rough swim, but finally I felt the bottom sweeping along under me as I pulled us toward the bank. I didn't try to stand up yet. I just kept holding the hair of his head and did a kind of swam crawl as the water near the edge got more and more shallow. Finally, we got to a back eddy in the water. I was nearing exhaustion when I was able to get a hand hold on a fallen tree along the bank and defeat the current still trying to drag him downstream. The drag from the big guy almost pulled us back into the current, but I finally got him into slack water.

It took everything I had to get the guy out of the water. He had to be 300 pounds of soaked, dead weight. I had to drag him like a sack of cotton, but I got him high and dry. I checked his pulse, nothing. He was a dead man. I had just pulled a dead man from the water.

In CPR training, they told us that nine times out of ten, when you have a guy without a pulse, they are dead and they are going to stay dead. That is why it is so important to learn CPR. You are that person's only hope. We were taught to do it, do it right, and do it as if your life depends on it.

Despite being absolutely exhausted, I began CPR on the guy. First, I pounded his chest really hard a couple of times. I checked for a pulse, nothing. I positioned he head to open his airway and checked in his mouth. I gave him two big breaths and began doing compressions. You have to do them really fast or they don't do any good. On TV it looks easy, but in real life, it is not. It will wear you out fast. It takes an amazing amount of effort to get a good compression, and every so often, you have to stop and give the guy a breath. This guy, I discovered, had something with garlic for supper. I did compressions for what seemed like an eternity. I was almost at the end of my strength when the guy coughs up some water and starts breathing on his own. He pushed me off of him and rolled over.

I collapsed. I fell to the side. I just had to rest. I felt like I had just run a marathon. The guy was rolled over on his side. He puked up a lot of water. We both just laid there, recovering. I'm not sure how long, but it was at least ten minutes we laid there just breathing, resting. I could hear the police sirens in the distance. I thought about how that usually meant that it was time for me to leave whereever I was. I knew that they were looking for the guy I had just pulled from the water. I knew that he was either the burglar or the cop, but I didn't really care which one. I had just saved a drowning man. He had been dead and I brought him back to life.

Catching my breath after that struggle, it was starting to soak in that I had just saved a guy's life. He was dead, at heaven's gate, about to cross the bridge. He had not been breathing, and I had saved him. Just as all this was happening, the last of the storm clouds moved out, and a full moon shined down upon us on the bank by the raging flood waters rushing past in the ditch. I looked up at the night sky. It was full of God's stars. The air was cool and there was a gentle breeze that gave me a shiver. The storm was gone. It was a great night to be alive.

Every few seconds, the last remnants of distant lightning lit up the guy, who was laying a few feet away in the shadow of the trees. He was a big guy. In the quick glimpses the lightning gave me, I could see he was still catching his breath. At this point, I relaxed some because, and I don't know why, I had concluded that the danger was past. H would be okay. He rolled over and turned to face me. I couldn't see him yet because he was still in the shadows, and I was in the bright moonlight.

He looked at me, then he shook his head. I could see him look closer at me. Lightning flashed nearby and thunder rumbled its warning.

A voice that I remembered oh-so-well greeted me. "Well, hello there, Billy Boy."

I dove back in the ditch.

The Valley of the Shadow

So, I dove back into the creek. That always freaks everyone out, but the truth is that seemed like the better option once I figured out that the guy I just pulled from the water and brought back to life was the big bastard who swore he'd feed my liver to the fish so many years ago. The water was my best way out, so I took it. Even if I wasn't entirely sure I could survive the water, I was pretty confident that he wouldn't come in to get me.

I got washed all the way down into Big Ditch. There was a big culvert where the creek went under the Highway 63 bypass that I didn't know about. Getting swept there was pretty scary and bangs you up pretty damn bad. It wasn't too long after that when the creek dumped into Big Ditch. From the culvert to Big Ditch, it was more like a waterslide at Six Flags Over Texas than anything else.

Big Ditch wasn't real turbulent like the creek was. Swimming in the creek was like trying to swim in a blender. Big Ditch wasn't that bad. It was just fast moving. Out in the channel, it wasn't very rough. I was pretty worn out again, and staying afloat was getting to be tough. I pulled my britches off, tied off the legs and filled them with air to make a float just like they taught us to in our water survival training with The Unit. Using the britches as a float, let me rest and get my breath. Once I had done that, I wasn't really in any danger anymore. I just went with the current for a while so I could put some distance between me and the big bastard. I needed the rest, too. Eventually I started trying to make my way over to the bank. Since the water was up so much from the flash floods, the banks weren't real steep. I managed to get to the side, and when I came past a fallen tree laying out into the ditch, I grabbed it and was able to climb out of the water. It sure was good to be on dry land.

Back in town, the cops had got in touch with the sheriff. They had cops and deputies all around Big Ditch watching for the burglar to go floating by. JD finally got a hold of Storm Center to tell them what had happened to me, but it takes so long for information to get shared that none of the cops knew I got washed away too. The cop who was chasing the burglar had escaped from the creek right after he fell in. He made it back to his car. He got on the radio and updated everyone that the burglar got washed away in the creek. By the time he did that, JD and I were already out of the truck watching for the guys in the ditch. The cops and the sheriff's men were all looking for the burglar downstream on the creek and out on Big Creek. They didn't really have a description of the burglar to work with. They were just looking for someone climbing out of Big Ditch.

When I emerged from Big Creek, soaking wet and exhausted, sheriff's deputies found me right away. I was barefooted, walking down a gravel road, soaking wet and wearing nothing but my Fruit of the Loom underwear, when I saw them coming with their lights flashing. I waved to them to make sure they saw me. They saw me alright. They jumped out of their car hollering and screaming for me to get on the ground. They had a dog with them. I was confused. I was glad to see them, but they were pulling down on me with guns. They turned the dog loose.

The massive dog came at me like he was shot out of a cannon. I braced, expecting to get knocked down and mauled by the dog. I was surprised as hell to see that it was Mickey. Mickey was a police dog JD and I used to feed Vienna Sausages to when we were on tornado drills. Mickey recognized me right away and rather than mauling me, got busy giving me sugar. Mickey loves me, but still he hit me at a dead run and knocked me down. I think it really pissed off the deputies because rather than eating my ass up, he was giving me some big-time love. The deputies took advantage of this and moved in. After stepping on my head a couple of times, they cuffed me and bounced me off the back of the car while telling me to stop resisting. They did a perfunctory search. It's pretty hard to hide a weapon when the only thing you have on is a pair of Fruit of the Loom jockey shorts.

I tried to tell them I wasn't the burglar, but they were not in a listening mood right then. They put me in the back of their car. When I say they put me in the back of their car, what I really mean is that they flung me into the door of the car a couple of times on accident, before they actually opened it and tossed me in. Kissing the door like that really made me see stars. They put Mickey in there with me. Mickey kept licking me in the face and I couldn't stop him because my hands were cuffed behind my back. I didn't realize it at the time, but beating my head against the door had opened up a cut in my right eyebrow. The dang dog was licking the blood off my face. I hope that dog doesn't have worms.

I was sitting handcuffed in the back of the deputies' car with Mickey licking my face which was still bleeding from when they tossed me into the door of the car door. My feet were bleeding from walking down a gravel road barefooted. No one was saying anything while the deputies made some notes. The only sound in the car was the dog licking my face. Just as the deputies were about to radio in that they had captured the burglar, they got an update on the radio. The dispatcher told them to be on the lookout for a white, teenaged boy, approximately five-foot-ten and 155 pounds. He is thought to have been washed into Big Creek along with the burglary suspect.

One deputy looked at the other. The one in the passenger seat looked through the wire partition and into the backseat at me. He had an oh-shit look on his face. Mickey was still cleaning me up pretty good, but the cut over my eye and the lump on my forehead said there would be no concealing that I had been roughed up pretty good. He picked up the radio microphone and in a very contrite voice, notified the sheriff's office that they believed they had apprehended the boy in question. No one said a word the rest of the way to the sheriff's office. I think they knew they were going to catch hell for bashing me around like that. I smiled. It couldn't happen to nicer guys.

When it was all over and done at the sheriff's office, it was a mess. In some ways it was a very, very good mess. Sheriff Floyd was one of Dad's oldest friends in Jonbur. It was he who had arrested me a couple of years ago because my science fair project was illegal. To say he was not happy that his deputies had roughed me up so much is not accurate. He was furious. He gave them an ass chewing I'll bet they never forget. Honestly, I looked so bad mostly because bouncing down the creek, through the culvert and getting blasted out into Big Creek beats you up pretty badly to begin with. I was absolutely covered in bruises, scrapes, and cuts. Sheriff chewed them out so bad that he chewed right through ass and got down to bone. I enjoyed that a lot.

Once he got that out of his system, Sheriff Floyd asked me a ton of questions about the burglar, and what had happened. I told him all about it with all the details that I could remember. I told him where it was that the burglar and I made landfall. I also told him about when I encountered the deputies and the dog.

After talking for about an hour, the Sheriff gave me some of the very best advice I've ever had. I thought it over as he was speaking, and it was absolutely brilliant. It's not often that I resolve to absolutely take someone's advice, but this was one of those occasions. Just as I was settling in on this, a deputy stuck his head in and said Mom and Dad were here. The Sheriff said to bring them on back to his office.

For the first time in I'm not sure how long, Mom was genuinely glad to see me. Neither she nor Dad knew that I had been out storm spotting, so when the police showed up at the house to tell them I had been swept away in a flash flood, it understandably caused something of a panic. Both Mom and Dad were happy to see me, but Mom was really concerned about how beat up I was. It seemed that more and more bruises were coming up, and more and more places were hurting. In addition to the cut over my eye, I seem to have picked up some fire ant bites and I had a rash coming up on my belly. Mom asked how I got out of Big Creek being so banged up.

I looked at Sheriff Floyd and smiled. The deputies had come in with Mom and Dad. They were looking none too comfortable. I smiled at them and said, "Getting blasted down the Ditch like that really beats you up. If Deputy Harris and Deputy Hound hadn't been there to help me out of Big Ditch, I would have been washed all the way into the Saint Francis River." In other words, I lied.

Sheriff Floyd smiled. The deputies smiled, and I smiled back at them. At this point, I knew that I would never, ever have any problems with a cop or a deputy in Craighead County, Arkansas, for the rest of my life.

We left and went home, but this wasn't over. While I was staying at Mom and Dad's house recovering from the trip down the creek, some began to doubt my story about the big bastard being the burglar. I think the doubt started when we went back to the place where I got him out of the water. High water had washed away any sign that we had ever been there.

There were no footprints or anything. Even the tow strap was gone. It was eventually recovered hung on some brush near the culvert before Big Creek.

The investigator for the Jonbur City Police noted that no one, not even me, ever got a good look at the burglar. Butterfield, the investigator noted, was last reported incarcerated on death row in the penitentiary in Mississippi. The cop that chased the burglar into the creek didn't get a good look at him. He just said the guy he was chasing wasn't really that big a guy, definitely not a huge guy. Keep in mind that the cop saying this played defensive end at the University of Arkansas. He was a two-year starter. There aren't a lot of people on earth that would impress him as being a huge guy. The investigator said there just wasn't any evidence to back up my claim. He seemed to think that I was having "a hysterical reaction to a near-death experience." He said I had probably come close to drowning in Big Ditch.

"It's really rough water, and it's more than a little surprising he survived," he said in a very serious and somewhat pompous voice. "Now, he is experiencing a hysterical reaction to it. I have seen it in Vietnam veterans many times," he said as if he were reaching a conclusion. "He may become a bed wetter for a while," he added. "It's sad, really."

"That man is an idiot," I thought.

Next thing I knew, I'm living in the basement at Mom and Dad's and I'm seeing Dr. Guntree again. The newspaper reported that the Jonbur police had concluded that my sighting, of the big bastard who kidnapped me, was a hysterical reaction to a near-death experience in Big Ditch, and that I was undergoing psychiatric care as a result. The prognosis, they added, was uncertain.

Assholes.

Dr. Guntree is the psychiatrist that Mom and Dad sent me to after Walt and I got expelled from Miss Black's School for Boys for hunting ghosts upstairs in the big house. He taught me that some things are reasonable and other things are not, seeming to imply that trying to save everyone at kindergarten from the onslaught of ghosts was not a reasonable thing to do. He never could wrap his brain around the fact that it was Miss Black, who told us ghosts were up there in the first place. He seemed happy to see me, but I certainly wasn't happy to see him.

I started visiting with him a couple of times a week, even after I moved back to the farm. I could tell no one believed me anymore about the big bastard. I knew that people were laughing at me. I could hear them whisper. Dezi, Walt, and

JD, were about the only ones who still had any faith in me at all.

Dr. Guntree was still easy to talk to. At first, we didn't even talk about the night it all happened. We talked about all kinds of stuff. He had heard about the golf cart crash, and he actually witnessed the wrestling match at the Country Club. He even said, in retrospect, he found that a little funny. He had given first aid to Mom when she fainted. I told him about what Sweet Pea said about good luck, and how I should consider getting religion so that my luck might change. He did find the dead mouse interesting, and he asked me if she still carried it. It's pretty chewed up now, I mentioned. I didn't tell him about Miss Lady eating it and dying. I didn't think he needed to know that. For the most part, Dr. Guntree really didn't say much. He'd ask a question and I'd talk for a while. He did take a lot of notes. I shared with him my concerns about my future. He did share his thoughts on that.

First and foremost, he said, having seen me play football, my future was never going to in professional football. I'm not going to lie. That hurt. How could everyone except me have known this? This was the second doctor who told me something like that. Just because it's unpleasant doesn't mean it's not true. I came to realize that the NFL really wasn't ever a good career choice for me. Just because you dream something up, doesn't make it a good idea.

Secondly, despite what Enid had said, Dr. Guntree said that I was not a convict. "Convicts are people who have been convicted of a felony and sent to the penitentiary," he said. "They are not kids who steal population signs and operate moonshine stills for a school project." He said that sometimes I maybe exercised poor judgment, but I certainly was no convict. I felt a lot better about that.

My "record," he said, certainly would not keep me out of medical school if that was the direction I wanted to go. Dr. Guntree said that no medical school would care that I had been jailed at eight years of age for mischief or that I had been arrested for my science fair project. In fact, because the science fair project was a moonshine still, it might even help me stand out from the crowd of other medical school applicants. That was good news I told him, but that I had never intended to go to medical school.

"A medical life is a tough life," I told him knowing that he would understand.

"That it is," he nodded in agreement.

Dr. Guntree was very, very adamant that I had many more career choices than just being a rodeo clown. "The world is wide open to you," he said with a smile. "All doors are open to you!"

Eventually, after several visits, he finally got around to asking me about the night of the storm. We talked a good long time about it. He was very interested in what a storm spotter does, so I explained everything to him. I explained the training we had, and all the gear we used. We talked about wind, and rain and lightning. We talked about all the precautions we took to stay safe. We talked about fear and how we react to it. We talked about how we control it. We talked about how exhilarating and exciting it is to be in an organization like The Unit. I explained to him is a lot of fun at first, but once you've sat in a truck that is inside one of those big bad storm cells, it's never just fun and games again. It's scary as hell. The wind rocks the truck, and the rain sounds like hail stones right up to when hail stones actually start falling, and then you know exactly how loud hail stones on a truck can sound. The lightning is so close and loud that you can't communicate over the radio due to the static.

"Why do you do this if it's so frightening?" he asked.

"The first time, you do it because it's exciting," I said. "But after that, you do it because it's important that someone do it."

Finally, we talked about what happened after JD and I heard about the burglary on the scanner. I told Dr. Guntree how we talked about where the creeks went and what they dumped into. "We figured it out pretty quickly," I said, "but we couldn't get through on the radio to give anyone the heads up."

"No one," I told him, "knew the ditches and creeks better than JD and me. We have seen fast water many times and we were pretty damn sure that if someone didn't get to the burglar and the cop quick, we would be recovering their bodies pretty soon."

"We were pretty sure that neither one of them," I said, "knew how to survive in fast water."

Dr. Guntree continued to make a lot of notes. He asked me about the rescue and when I got pulled into the creek. I told him the whole story with all the details start to finish. He listened very intently. Every now and then, he'd ask a question.

"Why didn't you just let him go?" Dr. Guntree asked.

"Because I knew I could save him," I replied as if that was a stupid question.

"Weren't you afraid of drowning yourself?" Dr. Guntree inquired. It sounded like he didn't believe me.

"Honestly, that never occurred to me," I said. "Once I stepped out in the water, I was focused on getting him out." I continued, "I know I broke the rules about hazarding myself, and that's why I got yanked in. Sometimes you have to break the rules to do what is right."

I looked at Dr. Guntree. "Once I was in the water with him, I could see that he had given up hope. He was in the process of dying," I said. "I didn't want to let that happen. I got him by the hair of the head. He wasn't going to drown if I could help it."

I paused, remembering that night. "I did the sidestroke going down stream to drag him out of the current. I don't think he was breathing because he kept getting knocked over face down in the water, and he didn't fight to turn back over."

"It was a tough swim," I recalled. "I remember being afraid I wasn't going to get him out quick enough. It doesn't take long for brain damage to set in," I cautioned.

"Interesting. How do you keep from getting choked on the thrashing water?" Dr. Guntree asked, looking me straight in the eye as if he were examining me for clues.

"Doc, as long as you are swimming downstream," I said, "the water splashes on the back of your head and not in your face. Breathing or getting choked isn't really a problem. Most folks try to go upstream, and that's why they get choked and drown. Your instinct is to swim upstream. You can't let panic get ahold of you. You have to trust in your training. You just have to swim downstream to get out. Mr. Grimmet taught us all this stuff in rescue training. Swim downstream and at an angle and you'll be fine." Dr. Guntree made more notes.

Dr. Guntree just looked at me.

I didn't know what else to say, so I told him, "Doc, when you got to do something that you are not sure you can do, you just got to trust your training, and just have faith."

Finally, he asked me how I knew it was the big bastard, he said, using my terms. "After all, you never really saw him," and Dr. Guntree continued, "you said he was in the shadows."

"Doc," I said, "that man sat twenty-five feet from me in a Mississippi courthouse. When the jury found him guilty of murder, bank robbery, and kidnapping, right there in front of God and everyone, he stood up and pointed right at me. He said, 'Billy Boy, one day I'll feed your liver to the fish and make you watch while I do it.'"

I paused for a minute to let that sink in some.

"I carry a .45 caliber Colt 1911 semi-automatic pistol everywhere I go," I said quietly. "So that when he does find me, I have an opportunity to give him something to think about. That night, on the bank of that flooded creek, that very same voice that spoke to me in the courthouse, spoke to me from the mud and the shadows on that ditch bank in the very same way. Only one person besides that big bastard has ever called me Billy Boy, and I know for damn sure it wasn't her. Doc, if I hadn't ditched my gun, we wouldn't be having this conversation at all."

"What happened to your gun?" Dr. Guntree said looking at me quizzically.

"I had to ditch it when we were in the creek. It was weighing me down. It was too heavy to swim with when I was saving him," I replied.

Dr. Guntree put his pen down. He looked at me intently. I looked back at him just as intently. Finally, in a quiet voice Dr. Guntree said, "It really was him. He really was there, wasn't he?"

"Yes, sir," I replied. "Yes, sir, he was and he's gonna come back, too."

Dr. Guntree's realization changed everything. Dr. Guntree spoke with Mom and Dad. They got Sheriff Floyd involved. Sheriff Floyd did something the investigator from the city police should have done. He called down to Mississippi to get the scoop on Hector Butterfield's status. He found out what I already knew. Hector Butterfield had won his appeal some time ago and was released with prejudice. That means that not only is he loose, but he can't be tried again. Of course, the damn newspaper didn't run this story at all.

With the question as to the existence of the big bastard answered, the next thing we had to figure out was what to do with me. Hector Butterfield, by virtue of the success of his appeal, was a free man and could not be retried for murder, bank robbery, or kidnapping. There wasn't enough evidence to charge him with breaking into the drugstore the night of the storm. The cop didn't get a good look at him before they fell into the stream. There wasn't even any physical evidence that I had rescued him. Yet, Mom, Dad, the Sheriff, Dr. Guntree, and I, all knew that he was here. The only reason for him to be here was to get me. More than that, none of us questioned his resolve.

We had a meeting at Mom and Dad's house to figure out what to do. Mom, Dad, Sheriff Floyd, and Dr. Guntree, were all there. Mom had some snacks out and Dad had his company bourbon out. He had two company bourbons. One was the expensive bourbon for folks he liked. The other was lousy bourbon for folks he didn't like. Tonight, he had the good stuff out. The first issue, everyone agreed, was how to keep me safe. Mom wanted me locked in the basement.

Sheriff Floyd was a little more reasonable. He pointed out that if I was in Jonbur, and Butterfield knew that I was in Jonbur, the very best thing for me to do would be to get out of Jonbur. Dad suggested another visit to Mississippi, but Mom put the kibosh on that.

"If you remember," Mom intoned, "Mississippi is where this whole thing got started."

Sheriff Floyd, scratching his chin, said, "Out at the farm is probably the safest place for him locally."

He paused and surveyed everyone for just a second, then he continued saying, "It seems obvious that Butterfield will try to locate the boy by finding where his Mom and Dad live. That's not going to be hard. He probably already knows."

He paused and added, "It's summer, so he can't locate the boy by staking out the school."

Again, he paused to see if everyone was following his train of thought. Sensing agreement, he proceeded, "The farm, however, is the curve ball. There was no easy connection to you, Doc, because, if I'm not mistaken, the farm is actually owned by Dr. Neal."

What he said made a lot of sense. Dad had a handshake lease with Dr. Neal on the farm. Dr. Neal owned it, lock, stock, and barrel. He paid the taxes on it. He paid the electricity. Everything was in his name, and there was no connection on paper anywhere to Mom and Dad at all anywhere. Dad handed him cash for the lease payments so that the Infernal Revenue Service didn't know anything about the deal.

Mom still didn't like it. She was very much against me living way out in the boondocks all by myself with Butterfield here looking for me. Dr. Guntree pointed out that if I stayed in town, I could be seen about town. That would make me vulnerable to being found. If Butterfield located me, he said, Butterfield would act.

Sheriff Floyd explained it like this. "It's a very good idea for the boy not to be anywhere near where Butterfield is looking for him. If the boy ain't where Butterfield is looking, then Butterfield can't find him or get to him."

Mom still didn't like it, but everyone finally agreed that living on the farm made the most sense. So, for me, it was back to the farm. I really felt more at home there anyway. Mom made Dad get a phone put in. I had the phone guy put it in the other trailer, the one I didn't use. I liked not having a phone. It was peaceful at the farm.

As the meeting was about to end, Sheriff Floyd pulled me aside. "The boys heard you lost your last one," he said as gave me another Colt 1911. "This is from Harris and Hound. They send their best regards too," he added. I noticed this particular weapon had its serial number removed. I asked the sheriff to thank them for me.

Summer kicked in, and having a year's worth of experience, I managed things much better this year than last. I got started early and got the fences in good shape. All had made it through the winter and spring storms pretty good, but there were a few spots that needed mending. I moved the cattle to our middle pasture for early summer grazing and kept the close pasture and the far pastures for making hay.

In the heat of the long hot summer, I had time to think about a lot of things. When you are out in the sun, sweating bacon grease, bush hogging on a tractor, you get a clarity of thought. At first, I was a nervous wreck looking for Butterfield behind every bush. I had a new pistol and I carried my rifle when I bush hogged or rode the fences. I still kept a really sharp eye out for him. It took a little while, but I got comfortable again. If he was able to sneak up on me out here, it would be my own fault.

Sadly, Dezi and I were growing apart. It's hard being apart so much with me hiding out at the farm. She came out and visited some. When we went out on a date, now we always went to Paragould or Walnut Ridge. We both knew we were growing apart, but there was nothing we could do about it. We both were sad about it, but neither of us knew how to talk about it. It's just part of growing up. I realized that she had interests that I didn't share, and I had interests that she didn't share. It didn't mean we didn't love each other, it just meant there was more to our lives than we really understood. She was still the beautiful girl who took my breath away, but we just weren't meant to be together. It was a sad moment when I realized I was never going to get to check her for ticks. Sometimes it is the moment you realize that something is about to end that is the saddest moment of all. That moment lingers. It hangs in the air like smoke from a sparkler, reminding you of the beautiful thing that that once was, but no longer is. In the time I spent sweating and working on fences. I figured out that though a broken heart is neither fatal nor eternal, it is nonetheless, very painful.

I came to accept that even though I still missed playing football, football probably wasn't really ever a part of my future at all. There's no place in a Veer offense world for a short, slow rollout quarterback. In retrospect, I was really thankful for having had the opportunity to play for a couple of years with a pass-happy coach in Memphis. We were undefeated and the city champions. Some folks play a whole career and never enjoy either of those achievements.

Sometimes just riding a horse all day can clear up your thinking on a lot of things. I worked hard and I thought hard.

I knew medicine wasn't my future. I knew that I was not the man for a job that consumes you the way medicine does. I also knew that I didn't want to be a cowboy, either. While ranching doesn't consume you the way medicine does, fixing fences in ninety-five-degree heat isn't really a big thrill either. One thing I did know for sure was that I had plenty of time to figure it out. Some folks know from birth what they want to do with their lives, and others have to figure it out. I just needed to figure it out and everything would be fine.

I guess most of all, I had figured out that I could handle it, no matter what "it" was. The big bastard might jump me from behind a bush one day. I can't stop that. When he does, he's gonna get a surprise that he won't like. I was relieved to know that despite all my missteps, mistakes, and screw-ups, I still had a future that was not limited to being a rodeo clown. I understood that growing up meant that, while I didn't like algebra, I still needed to learn algebra. I didn't have to like it, I just had to do it. It's the right thing to do. Figuring out that doing the right thing is more important than following someone's arbitrary rules doesn't necessarily make life any easier, but it does make some of life's decisions much easier. Understanding all this really eases your mind. I figured out that while yesterday may be a memory good or bad, tomorrow is always a promise of a better day. I guess it's like Miss Angel told me last year, you just have to have faith.

One day about halfway through the summer, I was over in the middle pasture on Thumbtack. It was late in the day. I was just cruising the fences when a cool breeze kicked up some. I smelled hamburgers. I knew that I wasn't anywhere near Ray's Last Chance, but it was the same smell. Ray's had to be three miles away, but I could smell those hamburgers cooking nearby. The sun was low in the sky, so it was near quitting time. Thumbtack and I turned into the wind and once more we followed my nose. We had to detour a bit to go out of the pasture through a gate, but I found the smell again without any problem We rode a pretty good ways through the woods on an old logging trail. The longer we rode, the stronger the smell, and the hungrier I got. My mouth was watering when we finally saw the old, falling down building. The sign, Ray's Last Chance, had rusted through and was laying on the ground where it had fallen. Lights were on inside the old bar.

I tied Thumbtack up in the same spot in the deep shade. I got him water. He relaxed some. He seemed to remember this place.

Inside, it was just as I remembered it. I hadn't been here in over a year and a lot had gone on. I remembered that I owed Angel for the hamburger and beers from the last visit. Just like last time, it was cold and very dark inside the little shack. I went to the same seat at the bar that I sat on last time. I put what I owed Angel on the counter. I waited for the voice to come out of the darkness, but the voice never came. Instead, an old man wandered in from the kitchen. He drew us both a beer and sat down next to me. He lit a cigarette. He looked as weathered as the building.

I looked around the familiar old pub. The lights were on in the jukebox. The beer coolers were nearly empty, and I noticed I didn't smell a hamburger anymore. I noticed the frosting on my beer mug was melting and sliding down the side of the mug.

"She's gone, you know," he finally said to no one in particular. "Said she was done."

"Yeah," I replied. I took my hat off. I wiped the sweat off my brow with my bandanna. The cool airconditioned air felt good. I looked around the place. "I kind of thought she might be."

Lightning flashed off in the distance. The lights flicked, and a moment later thunder rumbled.

Just then, for no good reason, the jukebox started up with that same damn Hank Williams' song that Miss Angel played last year. I smile a little and sang along in a whispered voice. I had, after all, seen the light.

"Storm's coming. You best be heading home," the old man said.

"I reckon so," I replied. I killed my beer. The old man walked me out and watched as I mounted Thumbtack.

"Think you'll make it before the storm sets in?" he asked as he scanned the angry clouds overhead.

"I'll make it," I replied.

"You sure? It's looking nasty," he cautioned.

"I'll be fine. You just gotta have faith."

Biography

William Garner was born in Memphis, Tennessee, and raised in Senatobia, Mississippi, Hernando, Mississippi, and Jonesboro, Arkansas. After having been asked to leave Arkansas State University, he eventually became a graduate of The University of Mississippi where he enjoyed skydiving, hunting, fishing, water skiing, scuba diving, music, liquor, raw oysters, boiled shrimp, football, women and occasionally attended class.

Following a thirty year career in Information Technology, during which he became a recognized authority on Unix Systems Administration, he has become a semi-retired nuisance. In addition to being the Pit Boss on his award winning competition barbecue team and writing novels, he has become a PADI Scuba diving instructor.

He is the father of two daughters and one son. His grandsons actually are Chaos and Mayhem.

He and his long suffering wife, Landi, now live in their new home in a small Florida gulf coast community. They are enjoying the good life.